MOSQUITO
on an
ELEPHANT'S

RUMP

A collection of articles, stories and quotes
by Terry Teykl

Prayer Point Press

MOSQUITO on an ELEPHANT'S RUMP

Mosquito on an Elephant's Rump:
A collection of articles, stories and quotes by Terry Teykl
© 2000 Terry Teykl
Published by Prayer Point Press
Compiled by Lynn Ponder and Janet Goff
Edited by Lynn Ponder
First Edition, February 2000
Second Printing, March 2003
Third Printing, March 2006

Unless otherwise indicated, all Scripture quotations are from the Holy Bible, New International Version © 1973, 1978 by the International Bible Society. Used by permission.

ISBN: 1-57892-103-1
Printed in the United States of America

To order, contact:
Prayer Point Press
2100 N. Carrolton Dr.
Muncie, IN 47304
(888) 656-6067
www.prayerpointpress.com

Dedication

This collection is dedicated to every church and
individual who has laughed at Terry Teykl's one-liners,
received his admonishing, identified with his passion
and implemented his teaching.

May God complete the work He has started in you,
and reveal His incomparable power
through your prayers.

Special Acknowledgment

In the course of what we do at Prayer Point Press, we rely heavily on the gifts and talents of several individuals who, though they are not actually on our staff, are valuable members of our team. Amy McAdams who creates sensational, imaginative artwork, Carol Wright who does some of the best print work in the country, and Cindy Lanning who is a master of page layout and design are all among this special group. Their contributions are priceless.

During the work on this book, Cindy Lanning and her family experienced both indescribable joy and intense sorrow over the birth and death of a baby girl. Though she lived only six weeks, Rachel Ann Lanning made an indelible mark in many hearts, including ours. We prayed for her and loved her from a distance.

Though words can not begin to express the emotions of such a time, the staff of Prayer Point Press would like to take this opportunity to appreciate Rachel's life and the delight she brought to Cindy, her husband John, and their sons, Johnny and Vince. She was special to us and special to Jesus. She went to be with Him on His birthday.

Thank you, Cindy, for sharing not only your talents with us, but this precious part of your life as well. Rachel will be long remembered.

CONTENTS

PREFACE

I've heard it said that when God has a big task He needs completed for the Kingdom, He has a way of calling the unlikely, underfunded, unsuspecting and sometimes even unwilling. Just look at Moses and David. So when the Lord began searching for someone He could use to stir up prayer among United Methodists and other mainline denominations "all across America," His eyes came to rest on Terry Teykl. I'll bet He even elbowed His Son and said with a chuckle, "This is going to be good!"

Terry was the perfect candidate:

1. He did not know any influential leaders within his denomination.

2. He was not a very good United Methodist.

3. He had no money.

4. He wasn't sure he wanted the job.

But when God branded into his heart the words, "Build the

church in prayer," Terry listened and obeyed. He believed God for the impossible.

During the 28 years that Terry pastored, God was preparing him for this assignment. He bestowed on him a special anointing in the area of prayer that was apparent both in his pastoral ministry and his life. As Terry faithfully built the Aldersgate United Methodist Church (College Station, Texas) on prayer, he began to be sought out by other pastors who wanted desperately to learn about those things which God was so obviously working in that congregation. He began receiving invitations to teach other churches about prayer rooms, praying for pastors, prayer as a ministry and mobilizing a church to pray.

Terry was also one of the pioneer teachers of "prayer evangelism," helping to restore prayer back to its original purpose. He taught about praying for the lost with unrivaled compassion and energy. His own church reflected his heart for soul-winning, registering several thousand converts under his leadership.

It was in 1995 that God called Terry out of the pastorate and into the Church at large. Resigning his role as senior pastor of what was, by that time, one of the countries most dynamic mainline churches, Terry "put himself in God's sling" which was aimed at starting a prayer movement in the aging, declining United Methodist denomination. God told Terry that He had not given up on United Methodists, no matter who else had, and that they could not only live again, they could return to their Wesleyan heritage of passion and prayer. But the circumstances said otherwise. The denomination was being torn apart by internal moral crises and was on the verge of self-destruction. It looked like "mission impossible." After sizing up the situation, Terry concluded, "I'm just a mosquito on an elephant's rump. What can *I* do?"

Four years and a million miles later, we have seen what one man can do when he responds in simple obedience and faith to the calling of God. Through Terry's book, *Pray the Price, United Methodists United in Prayer*, at least half of the 25,000 United Methodist pastors in the country have been directly affected by this prayer message, and this number continues to climb. Thousands of United Methodists from coast to coast are currently praying every Thursday at noon for an awakening in their ailing Church. We have seen God open door after door for Terry to speak at United Methodist gatherings, and He has granted Terry favor with many Bishops and key leaders within the denomination. Terry has, in fact, ignited a quantifiable prayer movement in one of the largest spiritual institutions in America.

But that's not all. In addition to heralding the message of prayer in his own camp, Terry currently serves on the National Prayer Committee, the Denominational Prayer Leaders' Network and the Wagner Institute core faculty in Colorado Springs. He is on the road every week, conducting Prayer Encounter weekends, helping people learn how to talk to God and praying lost souls into the Kingdom. He has committed his life and all of his gifts and resources to the mandate he received so many years ago, "Build the church in prayer."

Terry often says he feels like the Budweiser bullfrog—the one that used to go flapping across the TV screen during halftime with his tongue plastered to the back end of a beer truck. He follows after the vision God gave him for prayer with absolute abandon. He knows the thrill and the danger of being attached to something much bigger than himself, unwilling to let go, yet unable to control his own speed or direction. He is truly "flung for God" at some of the religious giants in the land, and together they are making a difference.

God is truly doing big things through Terry Teykl. And while we realize that he is simply a broken vessel (or a "cracked pot," as Chonda Pierce would say), we also believe that God's hand is on him largely because of four characteristics that are evident in his life.

First and foremost, Terry is a man of true prayer. Not self-serving or "showy" prayer, but honest, ongoing communication with God. Terry has one of those rare and intimate relationships with his heavenly Father that you can almost sense when he speaks, like a bride who talks about her fiance with confident and gentle knowing. He listens to God and hears His voice, and God speaks often to him. We trust his leadership and believe in his vision because we know that both are the fruit of many hours of silent stillness before the throne.

Second, Terry is a man of enormous compassion, especially for the lost. His burden for the Great Commission is a direct result of the time he spends pressing himself into the Father's heart. The same compassion that flowed through Jesus to lepers, tax collectors and even his own killers flows also through Terry to the sick, the ugly and the angry. He has an amazing ability to love the unlovable, and offer bountiful grace where the world would dish out only scraps of justice. "Can I pray for you?" rolls off his tongue as easily as "I'll have a number three." And the one thing that sustains him through the most difficult days of ministry is the knowledge that souls are written in the Book of Life because of what he does.

Third, Terry is a man of genuine humility. Few leaders, even Christian ones, exhibit this Christlike characteristic to the degree and depth that we see it every day in Terry. He approaches life with an "others" orientation, always encouraging, promoting and recognizing the talents and contributions of those around him over his own. He is never arrogant or proud.

Finally, Terry is a man of uncommon courage. He is a bold innovator, quick to take risks and embrace new ways, new visions and new territories. He fears God more than men. In fact, he does not fear men much at all, which is why he has a strong propensity to color outside the lines and upset the status quo. The truth is, he can not stand the thought of doing anything exactly like everyone else thinks it ought to be done. He has a special gift for finding the one growing edge of each audience and parking on it, all the while making them laugh and cry, so that days may pass before they realize they have endured a much needed spiritual spanking.

This book is a tribute to Terry Teykl and to the work that we see God doing through him. It is our gift to him—a collection of treasures that, in our minds, sets him apart and, at times, redefines "ministry." It contains many of the inspired, practical teachings that Terry has become known for over the past decade, and is decorated with the stories and humor that have won the hearts of thousands. If you look closely, you will see that it is an epistle of obedience and faith—a journal of serious ministry through a messenger who refuses to take himself too seriously. Most of all, we hope that you will find it a unique testimony to the creativity and grace of our sovereign Lord, who sometimes uses mosquitoes to make elephants dance.

MAKING ROOM TO PRAY

Several years ago, a woman I will call Janice signed up to pray in a prayer room at Airline United Methodist Church, which sits along one of the busiest stretches of interstate in Houston, Texas. She believed in the power of prayer, but she really did not think of herself as an "intercessor." In fact, she had never openly prayed for anyone outside of her own personal time with God.

During one of her first visits, as she was praying quietly at one of the stations, she heard a knock at the door and opened it to find a young girl standing outside, alone. "Excuse me, but they seem to need help," the girl said, pointing across the parking lot where two ladies stood together, crying. "Maybe you could pray with them," she suggested.

Janice hesitated for a moment, timid about interfering in a situation which she knew nothing about. What if they did need prayer? What would she say? Her mind went blank and her stomach began to feel queasy as she made her way across the pavement. Approaching the two ladies, she asked, "Is there anything I can help you with?"

One of the ladies began to openly share that she had just returned from MD Anderson Cancer Center, where doctors had identified a large, malignant tumor in her body that would have to be removed. She was to have surgery the following week, and her prognosis was shaky at best. Despite the comfort of her friend, she felt hopeless and frightened.

Admitting that she "had never done this before," Janice offered to pray with the two ladies. She said a simple prayer, asking God for comfort and healing, and for guidance for the doctors and surgeons who would perform the operation. When she was finished, the three women exchanged phone numbers and went on their way.

About a week later, Janice received a phone call from the lady for whom she had prayed. Almost hysterical with excitement, the lady explained that when she went back for the surgery, the doctors took one more diagnostic x-ray and were shocked to find that the tumor had completely disappeared! With no treatment or medication, it had simply vanished without a trace. Unlike her, the doctors were speechless.

The two women rejoiced together, both overwhelmed by the miraculous answer to prayer, and before they hung up, the lady said, "I'm just so grateful that your little girl saw us. Will you thank her for me?"

There was a short silence on the phone. "My little girl?" Janice questioned. "I was alone. I thought the little girl was with you."

I know that part of Houston, and I know that little girls do not just wander around without supervision anywhere near that church. I believe, as does Janice, that the little girl who knocked on the door was an angel. As Janice prayed in the prayer room, the Holy Spirit engineered a divine encounter so that God could bring glory to Himself through a miraculous healing.

What is a Prayer Room?

Jesus said, "My Father's house shall be a house of prayer." In other words, the primary activity in the local church should be to seek God and ask that His will be accomplished in our congregations and communities. Today we build "houses" for preaching and fellowship. Our churches have rooms for offices, music practice, youth events and meetings. We have places for the bride and maintenance staff. Yet when it comes to prayer, we have no room. The very thing Jesus told us to house, we make no provision for.

Many churches today, however, are correcting this oversight. Local churches all over the land are making room to pray. In fact, one of the fastest growing spiritual movements in the country is prayer room intercession.

So what exactly is a prayer room? Every one I have seen is different—some are big, and some are small; some are elaborate, and some are simple. They vary in appearance as much as church buildings do. However, most prayer rooms do have several things in common.

1. They are private. Churches have put prayer rooms in extra classrooms, unused offices, junk rooms, empty storage closets, portable buildings, chapels—just about any space that can be closed off from outside distractions.

2. They are comfortable. Prayer rooms should be inviting places to sit, kneel or even lay prostrate before the Lord and enjoy His presence. Comfortable chairs, carpet, tables, plants, adequate lighting, sufficient ventilation, pillows and wall hangings all help create a pleasant atmosphere.

3. They are inspirational and informative. I encourage churches to organize their prayer rooms into stations, displaying helpful information to guide people as they pray. For example, a prayer room might have stations for praise, thanksgiving, waiting, singing, petitioning and repentance. Throughout the stations, helpful information such as names of area schools, city officials, principals, high crime areas, gangs, hospitals and media sources help intercessors pray more specifically. Usually there is also a place designated for special prayer requests from the congregation, the pastoral staff and the community.

4. If possible, they are accessible 24 hours a day. Since most church buildings are locked when they are not in use, it is good for prayer rooms to have an outside entrance of their own with some kind of combination lock. They also need to be equipped with a telephone and good outside lighting so that safety is not a concern, even at night.

5. They follow some kind of schedule. While some prayer rooms accommodate many people at once and others are created for individual use, most are used on a sign-up basis. The goal of prayer room intercession, in most cases, is to have someone interceding in the room at all times.

Perhaps the best example in this country today of a first class prayer place is the recently built World Prayer Center in Colorado Springs. With beautiful hotel rooms, many individual prayer "cubicles," several conference rooms and classrooms, a seminar room set under a revolving globe, a war room for international prayer intelligence and plenty of the latest computer technology, this multimillion dollar facility stands as a powerful statement about the importance of prayer and its relevance to everyday life. The

World Prayer Center organizes prayer around the globe and will someday network local church prayer rooms across America. It is a hub of prayer activity, a milestone in the prayer room movement that has exploded over the last decade.

Advantages of Prayer Places

The prayer room phenomenon is not without biblical precedent. In Acts 1:14 we find the early church praying continually in the Upper Room. Around the clock, they came to seek God. They met there again in Acts 4. Later, in Acts 16:13, we see the apostles going to "the place of prayer." Evidently the early church had special sites for frequent and intense prayer. Today, we see many such prayer centers in Korea.

Thankfully, churches all over America are also providing such places. There are over 1,500 Southern Baptist churches with intercessory prayer room ministries. Many of these are 24 hour prayer rooms with telephone numbers to call for personal needs. The Kansas City Fellowship Vineyard Churches have rooms where prayer is conducted at 6:00 a.m., noon, and 6:00 p.m. daily. The Hillcrest Church in Dallas, Texas has a "house of prayer" where someone is available to pray personally for anybody in need who stops by.

In these unique places of prayer, people are crying out to God day and night on behalf of their communities for spiritual awakening. Jesus said, "And will not God bring about justice for his chosen ones, who cry out to him day and night? Will he keep putting them off? I tell you, he will see that they get justice, and quickly" (Luke 18:7-8).

Churches are simply taking closets or infrequently used rooms, and turning them into attractive and inviting places for prayer.

Here are some of the advantages to establishing a prayer room in your church.

1. A prayer room makes it possible to schedule prayer. In Acts 2:15 they prayed at 9:00 in the morning. In Acts 10:30 it was 3:00 in the afternoon, and in Acts 10:9 it was noon. Quite often, if we don't schedule prayer it just won't happen. Usually, members sign up for one hour in the prayer room weekly.

2. A prayer room promotes agreement in prayer by providing a place where information can be gathered and displayed. The assortment of information displayed in a prayer room can help intercessors pray more effectively and creatively. It also keeps everyone praying on the same page.

3. A prayer room offers a place to record the deeds of God so that we do not forget to thank Him and praise Him for all He does. The Titusville Baptist Church has kept an ongoing praise journal in their prayer room since 1972. Nothing inspires people to keep praying like real-life answers.

4. A prayer room sends a statement to the community about the importance of prayer. It can be a visible reminder to those with needs that someone cares and is willing to intercede. It is always exciting to drive by a church with a prayer room and see a car parked out front. I know that someone is inside seeking God in behalf of their city.

5. A prayer room provides a place where prayer can be practiced and matured. As intercessors come, the Holy Spirit will guide and instruct them as they get still before God. The layout and information in a prayer room can actually teach good prayer habits to those who pray around the stations. Some prayer rooms also have a children's area so that young ones can pray right along with their parents.

6. **A prayer room is inclusive, meaning anyone can sign up to pray.** It can be an inviting place for elderly people, young people and business people, and can offer prayer opportunities for both new Christians and seasoned intercessors.

7. **A prayer room can act as a "hearing aid" for church leadership.** Just as Jesus did, pastors and leaders need time to draw apart and listen to God. Often He will give vision and direction to those who are willing to wait patiently in His presence. The more time we spend alone with Him, the more He instills His heart in us.

8. **A prayer room provides a setting where major concerns can be "soaked" in prayer.** A big decision, a terminal illness, a major crisis, a special project—all of these situations would require heavy doses of long term prayer. Concerns like these can be placed in the prayer room so that they receive ongoing attention from intercessors.

9. **A prayer room ministers the presence of God in a unique way to those who come.** One woman told me, "It must be what the Holy of Holies was like!" In a society full of noise and telephones, a prayer room provides a quiet place where the Holy Spirit can work and be heard.

10. **A prayer room is a control center for strategic prayer evangelism, spiritual warfare and other prayer efforts.** It can serve as the headquarters for a city-wide prayer plan. As people come to pray, they take ownership of the church's vision to reach the city for Christ. Therefore, this battle is not left to a few or the pastor alone. Corporate repentance and seeking will invite revival and spiritual awakening.

Will You Make Room?

Prayer room intercession is powerful! God honors those who cry out to Him day and night, especially in behalf of the lost. He speaks to those who are willing to be still long enough to listen. Seldom have I run across a church with a vital prayer room ministry that was not growing and affecting the surrounding community for Christ.

Perhaps you would like to make room to pray in your church. Can you imagine people coming to your church on Saturday to pray for the Sunday morning service? If you are a pastor making hospital calls, you could tell a troubled parishioner, "I'll call the prayer room at the church and we will pray for you." Do you have a group of intercessors in your church who would pray regularly if they had a place? With some cleaning up and a little paint, can you picture that junk room off the sanctuary with people coming to pray eight-to-five? Jesus said, "My Father's house is a house of prayer." Is your house a house of prayer? If not, make room to pray.

(Originally featured in the January/February 1993 issue of *Good News Magazine*, titled "Why You Should Start a Prayer Room")

Tales and Treasures

Low-Hanging Fruit

"What can I get you to drink?" the young, dark-headed waitress asked.

Terry looked at her, ignoring her question. "Tell me something," he said to her. "Do a lot of people you wait on talk to you about Jesus?"

"Um, no, not really," she answered.

"OK. I'll have water."

The waitress disappeared for a few moments and then returned with drinks. "Are you ready to order?" she asked as she set the drinks on the table, obviously hoping to keep the conversation confined to lunch.

Looking intently at her, Terry asked again, "You mean to tell me that none of your customers ever talk to you about Jesus?"

"No," she said flatly, holding pen and paper poised to take an order.

"I can't believe that. I would have thought people bugged you about religion all the time. I'll have the chicken fried steak."

As we ate our lunch, nothing more was said about the waitress until she brought the bill.

"Was everything OK?"

Terry looked up at her one more time, sort of shook his head, and said, "Well, since no one else ever talks to you about God, let me be the first." He took a sinners' prayer card out of his pocket and handed it to her, saying, "I know you're busy right now, but when you get a minute, read that. It might help you. Everything was fine."

She took the dirty plates, the money and the card and retreated to the kitchen. A few short moments later, she reappeared and headed straight for the table. Looking directly at Terry with her hands on her hips, she blurted out, "All right, all right! I used to go to church every Sunday when I lived with my parents, but since I moved here, I quit going. But I'll go back. I promise! This week, OK?"

With a sheepish grin spreading across her face, she laid his change on the table, whispered "thanks" and walked away.

"Religion-mortis"

Those who attended the Aldersgate United Methodist Church while Terry was pastoring there know that every Sunday was an adventure. You just never knew what to expect.

One Sunday, Terry wanted to illustrate a point in his sermon about people who come to church expecting nothing and giving nothing. He called it "religion-mortis," a condition that created lifelessness in the pews.

Rather than simply talking about religion-mortis, and since he could not single anyone out as a living example for obvious reasons, he decided that his point would be well made by placing manikins throughout the sanctuary. They would no doubt raise curiosity and be a memorable visual aide.

So he went to a local department store, borrowed several male and female manikins, and dressed them up in church clothes. Early on Sunday morning, he sat the manikins throughout the church complete with Bibles, purses and other appropriate accessories.

"The plan," as Terry tells the story, "backfired. No one even noticed they were there! One of the manikins that was sitting on the edge of a row fell off his seat and the man seated next to him said, 'Excuse me.' An outgoing woman in the church approached one of the female manikins seated on the front row to introduce herself and was shocked when the woman's arm came off. Others, as they tried to find a seat, stepped over the manikins saying, 'Is this seat taken?' All in all, the plan didn't really work as well as I had anticipated."

I ride motorcycles. It improves my prayer life.

When you see something happen to someone at church that you don't understand, just say to yourself, "Isn't that interesting?" If you make fun of it, it will happen to you—in the hot dog section of the grocery store.

You're looking at me like a cow at a new gate.

What was my point?

Prayer is more caught than taught.

Every church has a junk room that could be turned into a prayer room. Just tell the pastor to office somewhere else.

The more successful your church becomes, the more you need to pray.

The power is in the tower!

PREYED ON OR PRAYED FOR

Someone said recently that modern pastorates look like the road from Kuwait City to Baghdad after the Gulf War—burned out and abandoned. As "point men and women" for the new move of God, pastors in local churches today stand face to face with the enemy's fire in every aspect of their lives. While they proclaim the gospel, Satan shoots fiery darts aimed at destroying their marriages, undermining their confidence, stealing their health, and tearing down their standing in the community. The attacks can come from outside the church or even from within the church itself, and fire from our own sheep can be the most deadly of all. As a pastor, I know this to be true.

Pastors have always had a difficult job, but the condition of the Church in this country today makes it even harder. Across the board, denominations are struggling to maintain their theological perspectives amidst declining memberships, moral crises, lifelessness, prayerlessness and disunity. In addition, the expectations church members place on their pastors are tremendous. George Barna lists the following in his book, *Today's Pastors*:

1. Live an exemplary life.
2. Be available at all times to all people for all purposes.
3. Lead the church to grow numerically.
4. Balance wisdom with leadership and love.
5. Teach people the deeper truths of the faith in ways that are readily applicable in all life situations.
6. Be committed to and demonstrate spiritual leadership in your family. Love your spouse and provide a positive role model for all children.
7. Keep pace with the latest trends and developments of church life.
8. Build significant relationships with members of the congregation.
9. Represent the church in the community.
10. Grow spiritually.
11. Run the church in a crisp, professional, businesslike manner without taking on a cold, calculating air.

Those are pretty high expectations!

Considering all that they have to accomplish and their role as generals in the army of light, pastors need to be prayed for so they will not be preyed on. They need to be blessed and protected by a hedge of intercession. I believe God takes it personally when people take His representatives for granted.

Recently, a prayer seminar I was scheduled to do at a church in the south was cancelled. I received the following note from the pastor: "Prior to the Aldersgate Conference in 1992 I was preaching on the person and work of the Holy Spirit. I returned home more determined than ever to preach for the renewal of the church. What I managed to do is to stir up both that which is wonderful and that which is ugly and painful. It is not the time for a prayer conference. There is much opposition to it. My future here is uncertain and I must be sensitive to God's backing one day at a time. I covet your prayers."

The casualties from Satan's war on pastors are all around us. Sex scandals in the church abound. Thousands of pastors each year are being removed or are retiring early because they are burned out. Divorce, and even suicide, are not unheard of tragedies in parsonage families.

Satan can be very creative, and he will do whatever he can to hamper a pastor's effectiveness. He may drop a bomb in the form of a major church crisis or serious illness, or he may simply chip away day after day until there is no resistance left. In either case, pastors are susceptible in several different areas of their lives:

Private and Family Life - With all of the demands that pastoring creates, it is easy for spouses and children to feel pressed, or sometimes even slighted, "for the sake of the ministry." And the pressure on pastors to maintain a perfectly wholesome family image is immense. When Satan attacks a shepherd's family in some manner, the results can be devastating because many shepherds are too afraid to reveal these painful vulnerabilities in order to get the help they need. Just as it would be for anyone, it is extremely difficult for a pastor to be effective on the job when one of his or her family members is suffering.

Praise and Prayer Life - Good praise and prayer time is what fills a pastor's spiritual cup. However, although pastors spend a lot of time at the church, they may struggle to find enough time to spend alone with God. When most of us are being fed during the worship services, our pastors are mentally sorting through details— Is the thermostat OK? Did I forget any announcements? I wonder if there are enough nursery workers? And is the baptismal ready? If Satan can keep shepherds worried over administrative issues, then he can cut off their power supply, causing them to feel drained and frustrated.

Professional and Preaching Life - Being a leader in any field is not easy, and leading a church is no different. It can be a treacherous balancing act to keep all the "groups" in the church happy, not to mention denominational leaders. Pastors can be pressured to compromise by politics and finances. They desire to be true to their calling, yet still want and need the respect of their peers. It is especially easy for preachers to fall into the comparison trap, measuring their success against the salary package and attendance down the street. The dart of fear, I believe, is Satan's most lethal ammunition in his war on shepherds because it paralyzes them to speak the confrontational gospel with boldness.

So why are pastors under such heavy attacks from the enemy? Satan knows, "Strike the shepherd and the sheep will scatter." He has been striking at shepherds since the first pastors of the early church began preaching the name of Jesus. Pastor Paul was shipwrecked, snake-bitten, thrown in prison, run out of town, beaten, stoned and left for dead—all for proclaiming the gospel. In Acts 20:23, he says, "I only know that in every city the Holy Spirit warns me that prisons and hardships are facing me." Barnabas, John and Stephen experienced the same kinds of persecutions in every city where they preached. The Book of Acts contains example after example of how the message of Jesus incited riots along with revivals. Jesus even told his disciples, "If they persecuted me, they will persecute you also" (John 15:20).

But something else is very clear in Acts. The early church members prayed diligently for their pastors at all times. They prayed for doors of ministry to be opened; they prayed for anointing; they prayed for protection when their pastors were threatened, and for rescue when they were in danger. Paul said in 2 Corinthians 1:11, "Then many will give thanks on our behalf for the gracious favor granted us in answer to the prayers of many." Jesus also modeled a way to pray for pastors when he said, "I pray for them . . . Holy Father, protect them by the power of your name . . ." (John 17:9, 11). If Jesus saw the need to pray for pastors, so should we!

God wants pastors to be fruitful. By praying the Word over them, you can make sure that they are blessed and protected. You can build prayer hedges around them by claiming scriptures in their behalf.

Do not expect shepherds to ask for prayer—they may not. Many pastors are reluctant to seek prayer from their flocks out of fear, or pride, or even humility. Some are afraid to reveal their needs; others may feel they are the ones who are supposed to have all the answers, therefore they shouldn't need prayer. Still others may think that they simply don't deserve special prayer when so many in their congregations are hurting. Take the initiative to begin praying for your pastor and the pastors of your city anyway. Your prayers will make a difference in their lives and ministries.

In order for your prayer hedge to be most effective, prayer must be deliberate and intentional. It will take time to develop, but be persistent. Here are some suggestions to help you begin to organize a prayer force:

1. Share your intentions with your pastor so he or she knows what you are planning to do. Be genuine, sincere, sensitive, and discreet. Ask for your shepherd's advice and concerns. Move slowly for long term gain.

2. Work with existing prayer ministries. Start by involving singles' groups or Sunday school classes. If your church has a prayer room, make sure it contains instructions on how to pray for the pastor. A few people could pray for the pastor while he or she preaches; others could pray early on Sunday morning. A team of trusted intercessors could maintain the hedge during the week. Be creative.

3. Recruit people to pray, train them, and then give them feedback. Start small and go for consistency and quality, building your hedge around those who are mature or already praying. Research several good resources on pastoral prayer and equip intercessors to do the job right. Don't overlook the mighty praying potential of shut-ins, elderly members, or children. Share the pastor's vision with those you recruit and encourage them by letting them know when their prayers make a difference. Give them a specific time frame in which to pray and as much specific information about the pastor's needs as possible.

4. Find ways to pray for other pastors in your city as well. You will reap what you sow.

In 1987, I went through a time of personal crisis and burnout. I was pastoring a large church, travelling frequently and trying to handle all the responsibilities myself. My life seemed out of control and unmanageable. At the same time, my church was going through several difficult staff crises, and I finally crashed and burned. Then I started to practice my own message! I asked people to pray for me, and I entered into a whole new relationship with my flock. I am convinced that I would not be where I am today without the prayers of the saints.

Praying for your pastor is your responsibility and privilege. As you honor your leader, you will honor God. Satan is prowling around like a roaring lion looking for a pastor to devour, and he attacks the most vulnerable areas of our lives. It is open season on pastors; and without prayer hedges we have little protection from the enemy who comes to steal, kill, and destroy. Will you be the one to stand in the gap for your shepherd?

(Originally featured in the January/February 1994 issue of *Good News Magazine*)

Tales and Treasures

A Window of Opportunity

Driving down a two-lane country road headed for a prayer event one beautiful spring afternoon, we came upon one of those scenes that makes you shudder. An eighteen-wheeler, wheels pointed skyward, lay in the ditch beside the road. Red and blue lights flashed all around the scene, as firemen, paramedics and policemen worked to secure the area.

We drove past quietly, whispering silent prayers for those who were involved. Several hundred feet down the road, Terry suddenly said, "Go back there." We circled around and came back to the accident scene to find that firemen had pulled a big, burly driver from the wreckage. He was standing, very shaken-up, beside the ambulance.

As we watched from the car, they put him on a gurney and began administering some kind of treatment.

Without saying a word, Terry got out of the car and headed straight for the man, ducking under several crime scene tapes to get to him. We watched him as he was confronted by paramedics and policemen, and to our surprise, they ushered him straight to the victim's side. He leaned down and spoke to the man and then pulled something out of his pocket. He placed it in the man's hands, which were resting on his bare, sweating stomach. With a few parting words which must have been a prayer, he returned to the car.

"What did you tell those policemen?" we asked, curious about how he had gotten through the lines so easily.

"I told them I was his brother."

"What about the trucker?"

"He knows God saved him from that accident for a reason," Terry said, "and he's going to read that prayer I gave him as soon as he is able. I think that big guy is going to get saved."

Neville the Undertaker

Early in his ministry, when Terry was pastoring in a small rural town, he actually worked part time for the town's only undertaker to make extra money. It was a known fact, however, that Neville the undertaker was a little "different." He worked out of his home. Once he prepared the corpses for burial, they would lay in state on Neville's dining room table until the day of the funeral.

Several of the elderly people in the church, particularly women, found this practice difficult to swallow, and they made Pastor Terry promise that when they died, he would not let Neville touch them. And under no circumstances was he to allow them to lay displayed on the infamous dining room table.

After the death of one such lady, some of her friends came to Terry on a Saturday night with a simple request, "The funeral is tomorrow. Can't we just let her rest in peace in one of the Sunday School rooms until then? We'll lock the door in the morning so no one will ever know she's in there."

Trying to be true to his word, Terry agreed.

The next morning, however, he picked up a little boy, as he often did, whose parents did not attend church. During the service, the little boy wandered out into the hallway headed for the bathroom, but stumbled upon the Sunday school room where the body was. Unfortunately, the door was not only unlocked, it was cracked, and the little boy could not believe what he saw! There she lay—hands folded, eyes closed, all dressed up with no place to go.

He didn't say a word about it though, until Terry took him home. As they walked up to his front door where his mother was waiting, she asked, "How was church today?"

"It's a great church, mama," the boy answered excitedly. "They even let dead people come!"

At my church, I used to have member-ship drives. I drove them all away.

I used to think spiritual warfare was a church board meeting.

I didn't mean to preach. It just fell out.

I'm from Texas. We just got English a couple of years ago.

We've sold our bullets to buy guns.

Trying to get unsaved people involved at church by asking them to serve on committees is like putting a flat tire on your car and hoping it will inflate as you roll.

Friendly fire isn't friendly.

The pastor is sometimes the least prayed for person in the church.

MOBILIZING YOUR CHURCH TO PRAY

Isaiah 43:19 says, "See, I am doing a new thing! Now it springs up; do you not perceive it?" God certainly is doing a new thing in prayer today all over the world. The interest in intercession and spiritual growth is on the rise, even in the "secular" culture. Churches are uniting within communities to bathe their cities and regions in evangelistic prayer. In the past few years, we have seen a tremendous increase in the quantity, organization, intensity and breadth of national and global prayer efforts. Whole denominations are mobilizing to pray, and organizations like the Denominational Prayer Leaders Network and the National Prayer Committee regularly bring together some of the world's most renown prayer leaders to collaborate and coordinate major prayer emphases. In short, we are revisiting the Book of Acts. If your church is not already mobilizing to become a part of this prayer epidemic, now is the time!

I was speaking at an intercessors' banquet at Englewood Baptist Church not long ago when I saw something that made a vivid, lasting impression. I walked into the sanctuary and saw a band of yellow cards that stretched around the entire auditorium. They were taped to the walls four and five deep in one huge, unbroken circle.

"What are they?" I asked Kay Bindrim, who is the prayer coordinator for the church in Rocky Mount, North Carolina.

"Each of those cards represents a prayer that has been answered through the prayer ministry here this year."

"How many are there?"

"I don't know, seven or eight thousand" she told me. "Maybe more. We know that over four thousand people received Christ in response to prayer, but there were many other answers recorded for needs other than salvation."

I thought for a moment about all the lives connected to those cards that had been touched by God because one congregation determined to pray. Thousands of cards—thousands of needs met and thousands of people won to Christ because of the prayer that went on in that church *in one year alone*! Most churches would be proud to record those numbers in a decade. Churches like Englewood in some respects define the cutting edge of the prayer surge that is currently sweeping the globe.

Of course, building a prayer ministry that will produce that kind of fruit does not happen overnight. It can happen, however, in any church that is willing to pray the price. And there is a price. Just ask Kay Bindrim.

When God called her in October 1995 to mobilize her church to pray, it was a "typical" church where prayer was concerned—they believed in prayer, prayed during the services, and had a prayer chain sustained by a handful of committed intercessors. Total number involved in prayer ministry: 20.

Today, they have eight vital prayer models operating in their church. For starters, 230 people are part of the "Prayer Warriors." Each one commits to come early on Sunday morning to pray for the services once each quarter. Next, the existing prayer chain was upgraded to cover any need in the congregation or from the community. Then they put in a prayer room, which is operational 24 hours a day and has 130 names signed up for regular weekly time slots. The "At Home Intercessors" group is an extension of the prayer room that is available to those like shut-ins, elderly people or single moms who may find it difficult to make the trip to the church every week.

In addition, the "Petitioners" ministry partners 120 teenagers in the church with adult sponsors who commit to pray for them daily according to the personal needs they share. The "Prayer Pals" ministry teaches children to pray while educating parents on how to incorporate prayer into the home. To that they added a cell phone prayer line that is available around the clock, organized prayer for the persecuted church, and a deacons' prayer team that ministers to the sick.

As if all of that was not enough, Kay Bindrim and her squad of staff volunteers have helped at least 32 other area churches begin their own prayer ministries, and they oversee several city-wide prayer ministries including "Ring of Fire," "Shield-A-Badge" and "Revival Candles." Total number of people involved regularly in prayer ministry at Englewood Baptist Church: 350. That is almost half of their Sunday morning attendance!

It is one thing to *say* that you believe in the power of prayer. It is completely another thing to *live* it.

So how did they get to where they are now? I guarantee it required more than just a halfhearted effort and an occasional, token investment. They worked, prayed, failed, prayed some more, worked even harder, failed again, prayed more diligently and kept moving ahead until things began to take shape. Then they really got serious.

What is happening there in Rocky Mount bears a striking resemblance to what happened centuries ago in cities like Jerusalem, Samaria, Damascus, Lydda and Antioch. The Book of Acts gives testimony after testimony of what happens when a group of people gets radical about prayer. The early church had no buildings, no board meetings, no hymnals, and no programs. They did not have litanies or an order of worship. Yet, as the disciples travailed in prayer, they made an impact on a world that needed God's love. They prayed to know and fellowship with God. With passion, they prayed to tell the untold, reach the unreached, and touch the untouched. As a result, they were empowered from on high and they saw unbelievable response to their outreach. They prayed—people got saved. Lots of people.

One common denominator between the prayer ministries of Englewood Baptist and the early church is the heart of God. For both, prayer was not an end in itself, but a means to bringing lost children into the Kingdom. They did not pray to get something *from* God, but rather to accomplish something *for* God. And because they prayed with the heart of the Father, He poured out His Spirit in response to their faithfulness.

Another common denominator is intentional mobilization. Englewood Baptist and the disciples organized themselves to pray.

So many churches I visit have dozens of ministries that are structured to the "nth" degree, yet when it comes to prayer, their strategy is, well, they don't really have one. They do not seem to know how to organize prayer for the sick or the needy. They have a hard time believing that a prayer room could really work. They think, "Pray continuously? That's impossible!" And the prayer they do muster up is same, lame and tame in the face of a society that is unraveling at the seams. It is crisis-motivated and short term. But it does not have to be that way.

Prayer can be organized just like any other ministry. You can have a plan, leadership, goals, recruitment, training, and feedback. You can pray in obedience to New Testament mandate with all the passion and purpose of the early church, and see thousands of lives transformed where you live! Let me share with you six important steps you should take to mobilize an effective prayer force in your church.

Step One - Begin to pray for a spirit of prayer to fall on your church. Gather together those who are already on board, whether it is one or 100, and embark on a consecrated time of seeking God and inviting the Holy Spirit. Ask Him to come like the wind and blow through every corner of your church. You might consider incorporating some type of fast into this preparation.

This step is critical for two reasons. First, you must take time to listen to God and receive your marching orders from Him. Do not rush out to copy something you have seen or heard about somewhere else. Let God design a prayer ministry just for your church. He knows the plans He has for you! If you will wait patiently in His presence before you make a single move, He will reveal to you direction, instruction, ideas, vision and resources.

Second, it is vital that you are prayed up because you will no doubt encounter resistance. Satan hates prayer and he will throw whatever he has in your way to stop you. People will come up with all kinds of reasons why the prayer ministry will not work— "We have never done it that way. We're too busy already. We don't have money in the budget." Be prayed up and don't give up.

Step Two - Establish leadership support. I can not emphasize enough the importance of a prayer coordinator like Kay Bindrim. A prayer ministry simply will not get far off the ground without someone who is committed to raising it up. And as soon as a prayer coordinator is in place, he or she will want to create a prayer task force or team to work with because the job is too big to conquer alone.

Prayer coordinators should be mature Christians, people of prayer, respected in the congregation and trusted by the pastor. They must be willing and able to give time and attention to the job. Most importantly, they must be appointed by God, and they must never, under any circumstances, be the pastor!

The pastor does have a vital role in mobilizing to pray, however. Few programs succeed in any church that are not encouraged, supported and even participated in by the pastor. As the leader of the congregation, he or she possesses the influence necessary to give priority to the prayer ministry and get people involved. The prayer coordinator and the pastor must be able to work together for maximum effectiveness.

Step Three - Lay the groundwork. As leadership takes shape and you seek God for direction, begin to assess the current prayer situation in your church. What is the attitude toward prayer? What is your church's theology of prayer? Are there any prayer models already operating? What about prayer ideas that have been tried in the past, both successes and failures? What other ministries in the church are especially dynamic? Could prayer become a part of those? Is there any place in the budget for prayer?

With these answers in mind, start working on a master plan. Establish some long term objectives and some intermediate and short term goals. Bear in mind that setting unrealistic goals builds failure into the effort. Include in your plan as many aspects of the process as you can think of like budgeting, resources, training, special events, promotion, accountability and maintenance. Both the prayer committee and the pastoral staff should have input into this plan.

Step Four - Teach. One of the most overlooked ingredients in a church mobilized to pray is a good education. First the prayer coordinator and team must invest some time in researching existing prayer resources. Then they must find creative ways to selectively filter this information to the congregation. This can be done from the pulpit, through Sunday school classes, in small groups, seminars or workshops, and by making prayer material available.

Unfortunately, many prayer ministries have fizzled out simply due to a lack of understanding. Most American churchgoers today, though they may have strong personal prayer lives, are just not aware of what is going on nationally and globally. They have not been exposed to the World Prayer Center in Colorado Springs, Colorado. They know very little about the millions who prayed for the 10/40 Window and the dramatic results that came about as a result of that initiative. I am sometimes amazed as I travel from city to city at the number of Christians who have not yet heard of prayerwalking or lighthouses of prayer.

Raising the level of awareness is what this educational step is all about. Expose your people to whatever you can get your hands on that will open their eyes to all that is out there in the world of prayer. Use any medium you can—videos, special events, testimonies, the church bulletin and newsletter, classes, posters and displays. Do not let ignorance be the roadblock to a thriving prayer ministry in your church. As people gain an understanding of the dramatic impact that prayer is having all around this nation and world, they will no doubt become more eager to participate in what God is doing.

Step Five - Implement prayer models. Here are some good guidelines to remember:

- You can not do everything at once.
- Do not expect to do anything forever.
- You have to start with something.
- Not everyone will want to do the same thing.

Start with one prayer model like a prayer room or prayer for your pastor. Once it is running and stable, add another one. Your ultimate goal should be to offer a wide variety of ways that people can be involved in prayer so that they can participate in an area that is meaningful to them. Remember to look for opportunities to connect prayer with exciting ministries that are already established in the church. Englewood took five years to develop their eight current prayer ministry opportunities. You will have to move ahead slowly, working for quality and not just quantity.

Practice "term praying." That is, always state when the time of prayer will begin and when it will end. No one can be expected to make an indefinite commitment, but they can always sign up again and again. This principle builds a sense of accomplishment into your prayer ministry because it enables people to complete what they start without locking them in until Jesus returns.

As you add new models, make recruitment, training, accountability, evaluation and feedback priority. Do not assume that people know how to pray just because they signed up; give them resources, guides and appropriate information. Equip those who participate in a first-class manner and give them plenty of feedback so that they feel confident as they pray and encouraged by the results. They will be much more likely to continue if the overall experience is a positive one. A little recognition never hurts, either. The intercessors' banquet in Rocky Mount that I mentioned earlier is something Kay Bindrim puts on every year just to honor those faithful people who pray.

Step Six - Maintain and assess. Chances are, you will make some mistakes along the way and you may even need to alter your master plan as you go. That is all right! Hindsight is indeed 20/ 20, so make use of that and be willing to shift gears if necessary. Churches are notorious for letting dead programs continue long after they have lost any sign of a pulse simply because no one has the courage to say, "Hey. This isn't working. It's time to let it go." Do not let sacred cows drain time and resources that need to be redirected.

On the other side of that coin, be persistent. Do not give up just because you run into obstacles or apathy. Remember that Satan hates what you are doing and he would love nothing more than to see you throw up your hands in discouragement. You must constantly be seeking the leading of the Holy Spirit.

As a final note, be creative and think simple. Nowhere in the Bible does it indicate that prayer has to be boring or complicated. Here are ten creative prayer ideas that could be implemented with very little money in almost any church:

1. Build a prayer library by collecting several of the hundreds of books that have been written on the subject in the last ten years.

2. Identify a prayer bulletin board in a visible place for announcements, requests, answers and general information.

3. Choose two other area churches each month to be prayed for during the worship services. Print the

names of the staff members and any special requests in the bulletin.

4. Organize a group of full-time moms to pray systematically for every school in the area.

5. Make a prayer calendar.

6. Take up business cards from church members and put them in a place to be prayed over for three months. At the same time, enlist a group of people to pray for the church finances using a prayer guide.

7. Send your pastoral staff to a prayer event or retreat for personal and corporate renewal.

8. Make prayer a theme for one semester of Sunday school.

9. Create a map of your city with helpful prayer information and distribute copies to all the local churches.

10. Put together a list of every members' name and reproduce it seven times. Label the lists Monday, Tuesday, Wednesday and so on. Each Sunday, ask for volunteers who will take one of the lists and pray over each name on the specified day that week.

As the disciples spent time with Jesus, they never said, "Lord, teach us how to manage the church finances," or "Lord, teach us how to develop a good children's ministry," or even, "Teach us how to win the lost." But they did say, "Lord, teach us how to pray." Become a praying church. Make a difference.

(Originally featured in the November/December 1994 issue of *Ministries Today*)

Tales and Treasures

Mistaken Identity

Terry was having dinner at a nice restaurant with a group of men following a prayer event. Since it was a Saturday night, nearly every table was occupied by groups or couples enjoying good food and company. But at the table across from Terry and the men sat a woman all alone. A little overdressed and heavily painted and sprayed, she appeared to be about 45, single and somewhat uncomfortable. She was large, but not obese, and her polyester rubbed noisily against her nylons when she moved. She was not especially attractive, but all the men at the table found it difficult to keep their eyes from wandering in her direction. There was just something about her that seemed puzzling.

Unfortunately, it was just the kind of situation that Terry can not ignore. He kept glancing at the lady, obviously distracted from the conversation going on at his own table.

"What is the matter, Terry?" one pastor asked.

"I just hate to see someone like that eating alone. Look at her. I'll bet she eats alone all the time," he said, stating the obvious.

The other men at the table shifted uneasily in their chairs, glancing at one another, until one of them piped up, "I wonder where our waitress is. Are we all ready to order?"

Once their food came, the conversation shifted back to the events of the day and what God had done through the conference. Terry seemed to have forgotten about the lady eating alone until about midway through their meal. That was when he saw their waitress lay the woman's check down on her table. Even the waitress's attitude toward this pitiful creature appeared to Terry to be abrupt and insensitive. He could not take it any longer.

"Ma'am," he called, trying to get the woman's attention.

"What are you going to do?" asked one of the men who probably saw disaster about to unfold.

"I want to pay for her dinner," Terry responded.

By this time, a couple of the men at Terry's table were doing their best to hide the grins that were taking over their faces. They looked at the woman, and back at Terry.

"What?" he said, finally perceiving that his companions seemed to know something he didn't. "What's wrong with paying for her dinner?"

"Terry," one of them whispered sympathetically, "that woman is a man."

No Habla Espanol

During a television interview several years ago, Terry was telling the show host about some exciting things that were happening among the gangs in their city. He was explaining that because of the ministry of one ex-drug dealer, he was regularly baptizing young gang members during Sunday services. One of the gangs that had been most affected was the "Primera" gang, which means "first" in Spanish.

Unfortunately, foreign language pronunciation is not one of Terry's strong suits, so he said, "Just last Sunday, three more came forward to accept Christ and be baptized! They were from the 'Primavera' gang."

Just call them the "Pasta Boys."

I don't do computers because they have a "cursor" button. I used to have a terrible problem with profanity.

. . . all across America!

You're looking at me like a dog at a new bowl.

How many of you used to be Methodist before you got saved?

Do you know why people don't go to church? Because they've been there!

There is more unity in the local bar than in the local church. For example, when sinners have a fight in a bar, they don't go out and start a new bar.

Prayer is God's idea and He makes it work.

You are writing Acts 29 where you live.

GIFTS OF THE SPIRIT

The young woman made her way to the front, watching her own feet shuffling forward on the red carpet. She knelt at the prayer rail, wondering if anyone could really understand her pain.

As Pastor Rutland approached her, he paused for a moment as a vivid picture appeared in his mind. He saw a young girl wearing a blue dress laced with white, standing alone on a porch crying. It was almost as if someone had flashed a photograph in front of him—a photograph which he knew nothing about. He knelt beside the woman and asked, "How can I pray for you?"

"I don't really know," she said. "I just feel so ashamed and depressed—I don't understand what's wrong with me."

Because Dr. Rutland is astute to the Holy Spirit, he knew that the picture he had envisioned was given to him by God. It was a snapshot from the Father's album—preserved for this moment of ministry.

As he described to the woman what he saw, she began to sob.

"On my eighth birthday, as I sat at our kitchen table with my parents and three older brothers, I opened a card that my grandfather had sent me. Inside there was a ten dollar bill. As soon as I pulled it out, my father reached over, snatched it out of my hands and gave it to my oldest brother saying, 'What does a *girl* need with ten dollars?!'

I was devastated. I ran out onto the back porch and stood there crying. My mom had made me a blue dress with white, lace trim for my birthday party, but nothing could make me feel pretty in my father's eyes. I hated him."

What amazes me about that story is not that Dr. Rutland was able to visualize such an accurate picture, but that years ago, the little girl's pain was recorded in the heart of God so that some time later, she could be healed. In His perfect timing, He found a user-friendly pastor, and played the tape back, supplying the tool needed at that moment for insightful prayer. What a loving God we serve.

The Right Tools

As the Church, we have an overwhelming task to minister to the needs of hurting people and to win souls to Christ. In an age of deception, racial prejudice, violence, rampant immorality, and broken relationships, we are still called to "make disciples of all men," a job that would literally be impossible without the proper tools.

I know a man who grows cotton on a farm of several hundred acres, and I went to visit him. I asked him to show me how all that cotton was harvested, and he allowed me to ride on his cotton picker with him. By hand, he could only pick a few pounds of cotton a day, but the cotton picker harvests several hundred pounds in just a few hours. For him, the right tool is essential to his life.

As Christ's representatives, the tools we need to carry out His work are known as the "gifts of the Holy Spirit." Without these tools in full operation, we would be harvesting souls "by hand" instead of using the resources God has available for us. The gifts of the Holy Spirit are our tools to win souls. They are as essential to our lives as the cotton picker is to the farmer.

In Acts 2, the apostles received the gifts of the Spirit to empower them to preach the gospel, and the results were astounding! Every time they preached, many believed and were saved. Everywhere they went, they caused both revivals and riots. The good news is, the tools did not die with the apostles; they were, and still are given by the Spirit so that God will be praised and glorified. First Peter 4:10 says, "Each one should use whatever gift he has received . . .," and Romans 12:6 tells us that we are all given "different gifts, according to the grace given us." The gifts are our tools—they are the abilities of Jesus inspired in us by the Holy Spirit to minister to a hurting world and bring people to Christ.

Although not everyone agrees completely on what all of the gifts are, most people look to Romans 12:6-8, 1 Corinthians 12:8-10, 28 and Ephesians 4:11 as references. In this article, I will address sixteen of the gifts listed in one or more of these passages: wisdom, knowledge, discernment, faith, healing, miraculous powers, service, mercy, giving, teaching, exhortation, leadership, prophecy, apostle, evangelist and pastor.

Intuitional Tools

Wisdom, Knowledge and Discernment

Finding your own spiritual gifts and learning to use them is so important. Many in the church have been given intuitional tools: wisdom, knowledge, or discernment, and they can use their tools to help keep the body on track. Wisdom is the plumb line of God, necessary to shoot straight and avoid being misled. Through wisdom, the Holy Spirit shows us how to apply the scriptures to our lives in specific situations. I consult leaders in my church that I know are gifted in this area before making major decisions because I trust their ability to hear God and stay focused on him.

I think of the gift of knowledge as a stud finder, making clear something that we could not otherwise see. It is the ability to see things as God sees them, and know things you could not know except that the Holy Spirit reveals them to you. He may impress a word upon your heart or put a picture in your mind. It is really not spooky or weird; why shouldn't God communicate with us like this? This tool is extremely useful in ministering to people with specific needs.

Knowledge is one of my spiritual tools, and I am still learning to use it. The first time God used me in this way, I was closing a Sunday morning service when He spoke the word "shingles" to me. Now I am not very smart, but I'm reckless, and I think that is why God uses me as He does. I thought, "Shingles. There must be a roofer here who needs to be saved." So I prayed for every roofer in the building. When no one responded, it occurred to me that maybe someone needed to be healed of shingles, so I tried again. When no one came forward for healing, I felt a little silly, and figured I had just really missed God this time. But after the service, a young woman came to me, and in a shaky voice, told me that she suffered from a rare form of shingles that is stress-induced, and that she was so stunned that God would single her out, she had not been able to speak up. We prayed for her and she experienced relief from her condition. In spite of my inadequacy, God handed me the right tool at the right time to minister healing, and He was glorified. None of us will ever become proficient with our tools if we are afraid to make mistakes.

Discernment is probably best described as a wife in your life who warns you before you do something foolish. My wife has the gift of discernment, and on several occasions she has used that gift to protect me from a situation that could have been very harmful. For example, one evening I received an urgent call from a woman in my church who told me she had just taken an overdose of sleeping pills to end her life. She sounded desperate, like one who is hanging on to the last thread of hope. She begged me to come right away.

As I explained the call to my wife, I picked up my car keys and headed for the door. But just as I turned the knob, she said, "Wait. I think I need to go with you."

When we arrived at the woman's house, the front door was already ajar. We knocked our way in and found her lying on the sofa—scantily clad and amazingly coherent for one who had taken an overdose of sleeping medication. She seemed a bit surprised that I was not alone. I returned to the car and waited while my wife counseled and prayed with her.

Discernment protected me from a snare that night. Like an X-ray machine, discernment gives us divine insight into people and situations. It enables us to sift through the stuff life throws our direction and sometimes avoid potential trouble.

Harvesting Tools
Faith, Healing and Miraculous Powers

Another group of spiritual tools in God's tool box are especially effective for harvesting souls into the kingdom. Faith, healing, and miraculous powers harvest like the cotton picker, by bringing God's power on the scene in such a way that His glory is revealed and His name is exalted. We are surrounded by people who need to discover and experience the meaning of the cross. Even our churches are filled with hurting, depressed, oppressed people whose hope has been snuffed out by the harsh realities of life. They need a touch from God!

Many of my members are committed to winning our city for God, and they pray diligently, claiming their neighborhoods and workplaces for Him. One young college student had a vision for his dorm to become a shining light for Christ on the Texas A&M campus. He knew in his heart that God was going to do it, and he believed for it faithfully in prayer. He never wavered. That is the gift of faith—an absolute assurance that God will do what he promised. Every church budget committee needs at least one member with this gift! Those who operate the faith tool effectively are like the energizer rabbit—they just keep going and going and going. And they will motivate others to do the same.

The gifts of healing and miraculous powers seem to be often misunderstood and somewhat controversial. However I know that they are real and for today, and I desire that they play a vital role in my ministry.

Jesus instructed his disciples in Matthew 10:6-8, "Go rather to the lost sheep of Israel. As you go, preach this message: 'The kingdom of heaven is near.' Heal the sick, raise the dead, cleanse those who have leprosy, drive out demons. Freely you have received, freely give." He told them also to "believe on the evidence of the miracles themselves." He said, "...anyone who has faith in me will do what I have been doing. He will do even greater things than these.... I will do whatever you ask in my name, so that the Son may bring glory to the Father" (John 14:11-13). Miracles were a vital part of Jesus' ministry on earth, and as branches on the vine, we are to bear the same fruit. We can never take the credit for signs and wonders, though, because we are not the source.

We simply show up on the scene, tuned in to the Holy Spirit, and he hands us the tool we need for the job.

Early in my career, in a small Texas town, I began to learn how the Spirit bestows on us these "gracelets," as John Wimber calls them. I was pastoring in Kosse and working my way through seminary. There were two brothers in town—hot-tempered trouble makers—who frequently visited my house at odd hours in the morning shooting off guns or yelling obscenities. I believed it was my job to save them both.

One night at 1:00 am, they knocked on my door, staggering drunk, and I let them in. They had just seen the movie *The Exorcist*, which had apparently terrified them. My wife and I realized that this might be a good opportunity to share Jesus with these two men, but they were so drunk, they would not have remembered anything. So we prayed for a miracle—instant sobriety. I have never seen anything like it. Their eyes became focused, their speech cleared up, and they sort of shuddered as they gradually became aware of their surroundings.

I would like to say that they are both serving as deacons in the local church now, but I do not think that is the case. I do know, however, that God got their attention long enough that night for us to present the gospel of Jesus Christ to them. God wanted a seed to be planted, and he gave us the ability to pray for a miracle so that we could do the job.

Helping Tools
Service, Mercy and Giving

Many are gifted with what I call helping tools—gifts that often bind the body of Christ together like a family. Some are gifted to serve by meeting practical needs for others. They tend to remember people's likes and dislikes, and are often willing to make personal sacrifices to help when necessary. This gift operates so strongly in me that my church leaders hide the checkbook from me because I will give anyone with a good story all the money in the bank. To find the servers in your church, visit the nursery on Sunday morning, or hang around after a Wednesday night supper and see who is cleaning tables and stacking chairs.

Working alongside those who serve are usually those with the gift of mercy. The Holy Spirit gives them deep compassion for people who are hurting or troubled. For example, the Society of St. Stephen, an outreach to needy families in our area, is run by those gifted with mercy. Would that the church today be characterized by compassion!

I tell my members that if they are unsure about what their spiritual gifts might be, to claim giving as one of them. Pastors would all love to have a congregation full of givers! Not only do these people give financially, but the Holy Spirit has also placed in them the ability to make wise investments, manage resources, and motivate others to give.

Finishing Tools

Teaching, Leading, Exhortation and Prophecy

Finishing tools are the ones we need as Christians to help mold and shape each other more to the likeness of Christ. Teachers are like a caulking gun, putting mortar between the bricks by imparting knowledge and helping to maintain discipline in the church. Leaders are gifted to organize and oversee, and exhorters or encouragers prod us along the way to finish the race and not lose heart. Barnabas was an encourager, and God used him especially in Paul's life during his early days in the church.

One last finishing tool that I believe is critical to the well-being of local churches is that of prophecy. Prophets are like surveyors who can accurately set our course and then warn us if we start to stray.

A surveyor's tool is called a transit, and it is the oldest tool known to man. No buildings are built, no property lines drawn, no roads or bridges are laid out without the skill of an expert surveyor. He sets his transit over a benchmark in the city, and whatever is to be built is positioned in relation to that point. If the surveyor for a new highway is off even by the slightest degree at the start, the highway would miss its intended destination by hundreds of miles! The surveyor must be very precise and very adept with his tool.

Likewise, a prophet, or "seer," must be absolutely accurate, and most importantly, must have his transit set on the benchmark of Jesus so that everything we do is grounded in him. When my staff has an important decision to make concerning the direction we are to go, we consult with the prophets in our church who can counsel us wisely. We are careful who we recognize as having this gift because when it is misused, the long term effects can be staggering.

Ministering Tools
Apostles, Evangelists and Pastors

Finally, we need to seek out and encourage those in the body who are gifted to care for and strengthen the flock—the apostles, evangelists and pastors. Apostles and evangelists work together as soul-winners and visionaries. They are often the sparkplugs who will ignite revival and motivate others to use their tools to spread the gospel. People tend to cluster around the apostles and evangelists, as well as the prophets and leaders, because their gifts are complimentary, and they need each other to reach their full potential. The more interdependent we become, the more we can glorify Jesus as a body since none of us possess all the spiritual tools. None of us have a tool box big enough to handle that much power!

Pastors, of course, care for the flock and oversee the body. Traditionally, pastors ministered and the people received. But I see this changing as Christians begin to do the ministering and pastors act as facilitators. If we are to win the entire world for Christ, we must operate this way.

Warning Label

These spiritual tools really should come with a warning label because with them come the risks and dangers that always accompany high powered equipment. They are one hundred percent safe and effective when used the way God intended, but unfortunately we are not always able to do exactly that. The skills necessary to use them take time and practice to develop, and sometimes we get careless. Misuse, abuse, jealousy and pride in the application of spiritual gifts can cause great harm and create an attitude of mistrust and rejection toward the whole idea. Irresponsible use of the spiritual gifts can even cause people to fear the Holy Spirit Himself.

However, throwing out the tools is not the answer! We need them to win our world for Christ and they are not the problem. All ministry in the church, including the use of spiritual gifts, needs to be carried out with order and discipline.

A man in my church accidentally cut one of his fingers off one afternoon while using a handsaw in his garage workshop. He had been working all day and was tired. He got careless. We called together a group of men to pray for him as he was taken to the hospital for repair, and he has since regained full feeling and movement. But as I sat in the waiting room, I imagined the headline in the paper the next day, "College Station Man Cuts Off Finger with Handsaw—All Handsaws Banned." How ridiculous that would be! And yet that is exactly what we have done with some of the spiritual tools—banned them from use because someone got careless. What a tragedy.

In order to avoid spiritual injury, one important precaution is the understanding that the tools should never draw attention to themselves or even to the workers, but should always reflect honor and glory back to God through the result. Their function is to minister to the needs of people so that Jesus' name will be praised, not to say, "Look at me. Look at what I can do!" If the focus is not on Jesus, red flags should go up.

Another precaution we can take is to learn the significance of each gift in the body and how they compliment each other. Because we are all gifted in different areas, as a church we are dependent on each other to be complete in ministry. We get in trouble when we become dissatisfied with the gift we have, when we put down someone else's gift, or when we try to force our gift on others.

In order to build a house, a builder must hire carpenters, plumbers, electricians, bricklayers, painters, and roofers. The skills of each one are necessary for progress to be made, and none is more important than the other. The carpenter does not try to do the work of the plumber, and the painter does not expect the bricklayer to use his painting tools. They work in harmony, and the reward is in the finished product. How much more effective could the church be in making disciples if we adopted the same attitude and worked in harmony together, respecting each other's different gifts and using our own to their fullest potential?

Some day, we will all stand before Jesus to answer his question, "What did you do with what I gave you?" As Christians, how many of us are just sitting on our tool box, watching passively while others are working to make disciples? I believe God grieves when we keep the gifts he has given us locked up, instead of using them for the work they were intended to do. Get off your tool box, and find out what is in there. The Holy Spirit has inspired in all of us the abilities of Jesus to equip us for the most exciting task on earth. What are we doing with what he gave us?

(Unpublished, 1995, Based on the tape series *Gifts of the Spirit*)

Tales and Treasures

A Holy Hunch

While on an airplane on his way to preach in a church in San Diego, Terry decided to pass the time by praying for the people sitting around him. Not wanting to talk much, he would zero in on one of his fellow passengers, and then lay his head back in the seat and pray whatever came to mind.

After praying for two little boys and an older gentleman, he noticed a young woman in the seats directly in front of him. He leaned back and began to pray for her. As he was praying, God spoke to him as He sometimes does, saying, "Everything will be OK. Tell her that everything will be OK."

With the seat belt sign on and the flight attendants rolling carts up and down the aisle, Terry decided it was best to wait until he got off of the plane so that he could explain his message to the woman without embarrassing her in front of strangers. But the Lord never stopped prompting him, "Tell her that whatever it is she is worrying about will be OK."

Finally at the baggage claim area, Terry had a chance to speak to the woman. "I'm a pastor," he explained, "and while we were on the plane, I think God told me to tell you something."

"All right," she said, a little uneasily.

"I'm not sure what this means to you, but He kept impressing upon me that 'everything is going to be OK.' Whatever you are worrying about will work out."

She thought for a moment about what he said, took a breath as if she was going to say something back, but then stopped herself. "Thank you," she said simply. "I think my ride is here."

The next morning when Terry stood up to preach, the sanctuary was full. But about halfway through his sermon, he noticed the young woman from the airplane seated in the very back. "What a coincidence," he thought, "that she goes to church here."

At the end of the message, Terry gave an invitation for anyone who needed to know Jesus to come to the altar. The woman immediately headed down the center aisle and stopped right in front of him.

"Hello again," he said.

"I have to thank you for speaking to me yesterday. I'm sorry I didn't really respond, but I was so over-whelmed, I didn't know what to say. As I was sitting on the plane, all I could think about was what would happen to me if I died. I'm terrified of flying, and I didn't know if God was real. I kept asking Him to show me if He cared."

"How long have you been coming to this church?" Terry asked.

"Well that's another funny thing. I never have been

here before today, but I pass by this place all the time on my way to work. After you spoke to me yesterday, I decided to come here and see if I could find some answers. I was astonished to see you. Do you think maybe God's trying to tell me something?"

Terry laughed. "Can I pray with you?"

The Wrong Color

Following a prayer event in a small town, Terry went to eat with some friends who lived locally. It was a nice restaurant and he wanted to join his companions in having a glass of wine with his dinner, but he felt self-conscious about it. He had already seen several people who had attended the conference, and he did not want to offend anyone.

So when the waiter came to their table, and it was Terry's turn to order his drink, he said, "I'd really like a glass of Chardonnay also. But I would like mine in a coffee cup."

"In a coffee cup?"

"That's right," Terry repeated. "In a coffee cup."

The waiter disappeared into the kitchen and came back with three glasses of wine, one of which was in a beautiful, clear crystal coffee cup.

I am on my 53rd day of starting
a three-day fast.

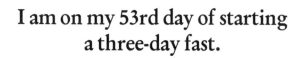

Is there a Starbucks in this town?

Some of you are saying, "We don't do
this in my church." Well, you're not
in your church.

Look at your neighbor and tell them,
"This wasn't as bad as I thought it
would be!"

Sinners are confused. How can we show them that God is love if we don't even like each other?

Get in His sling and let Him fling you.

I'm still a Methodist because we're going to heaven first. The Bible says so: "The dead in Christ shall rise first."

God just wants His kids home.

ACTION AT THE ALTAR

The Need For Personal Ministry

Several months ago, I boarded a plane in San Diego to return home, and found myself seated next to a very sharp looking, young man who was working on a laptop computer. Everything about him was a mark of success from his expensive looking, neatly pressed suit to the confident way he smiled and nodded when I sat down. I learned that he was the leading salesman in his company, and that he was on his way to make a presentation that could earn a high dollar account. I told him I was a pastor. He seemed eager to talk about his work, and since I had nowhere to go, I listened.

After several minutes, something he said prompted me to ask how long he had been married, and for the first time since I got on the plane, he hesitated to answer as his gaze fell to the floor. He looked up slowly and said, "Almost three years. My wife has cancer. She was diagnosed shortly after we were married, but she seemed to be doing fine until several weeks ago. That's when they found the cancer in her lungs."

Before we got off the plane, I asked the man if I could pray for him and his wife, and I told him I would put their names in our prayer room to be lifted up daily by intercessors. I cannot begin to explain the peace that came over him. As I left the airport, my heart was burdened for this young couple and the battle they were facing, but I was equally troubled by something else he said. Although they had been regularly attending a church there in San Diego since they were married, *they had never received personal ministry through prayer!*

Not long after that, a lady walked into my office early one Sunday morning looking very troubled. She closed the door, sat down on the couch, and pulled a small handgun out of her purse. She had my full attention. She told me that she was extremely depressed, and that her situation was so bad she could find no reason to go on living. She said that she did not really want to die, but she needed someone to give her hope. I was her last resort.

That lady was not interested in baking pies for a potluck supper, or in joining the United Methodist Women's group. And the man on the plane from San Diego probably did not really care whether his church sprinkled or dunked. I doubt either one of them would have found much comfort in a sermon that outlined the Council of Bishops political views on immigration. What they both needed was to feel the love of Jesus from the tops of their heads to the bottoms of their feet. Every Sunday, our churches are filled with people who are being run over by life. They wear a smile on their face to hide the hurt of marital problems, abusive relationships, children who have turned away, financial failures, and terminal illnesses. Our society is coming unraveled at the seams—plagued with violence, crime, immorality, homelessness, and hopelessness—and we all bear the scars. How tragic it is that broken people often pass through our doors and receive nothing but a bulletin and nice three-point sermon! They come to church, week after week, desperately needing a touch from God, and often leave in the same condition as when they arrived.

A House of Prayer

The day that Jesus drove the money changers and tax collectors from the temple in righteous indignation, he must have been very displeased with what was taking place there. But I believe He was just as displeased, if not more, with what was *not* taking place there. I can just imagine Jesus approaching the temple, stepping over the lame and the lepers, pushing His way through the blind and the afflicted, all of whom had come hoping for a touch and a prayer, but had received nothing. As He turned over the tables and drove out those who were buying and selling, He said to them, "My house will be called a house of prayer...." And as soon as Jesus had cleared the temple, Matthew says, "The blind and the lame came to him..., and he healed them" (Matthew 21:14). Jesus wanted people to be ministered to personally. He wanted His people prayed for.

If we are trying to impact our cities and communities for Jesus, we must be relying on prayer to see any results. Evangelistic efforts will be fruitless unless they are preceded by and based on prayer for the lost. It is important that we learn to pray for the felt needs of unbelievers so that as those needs are met, we can point them to Jesus, their provider. As Christians, we must find ways to pray with each other for the salvation of our cities. This kind of organized prayer force must begin in the local churches and it needs to start at the altar.

Why Altar Ministry Doesn't Happen

If Jesus modeled prayer as a ministry, and God instructed us to be houses of prayer, then why doesn't more personal ministry through prayer happen at church? What keeps us from doing that which both the Father and Son repeatedly emphasized as fundamental?

After visiting hundreds of churches and talking with pastors and their congregations, I have heard a variety of explanations as to why altar ministry does not happen. Here is a list of the top ten:

1. Nothing will happen. What if the pastor makes an altar call and no one comes forward?

2. Something might happen. What if someone starts to cry or makes a scene? What will the visitors think? What will we do to entertain the rest of the congregation while the altar ministry takes place? What if it gets out of control?

3. We do not have an altar.

4. We do not want to have to deal with "kooks"— those unstable people in every church who would want to pray or be prayed for.

5. No one really knows how to get it started or make it happen.

6. There is not enough time in the worship service. With two Sunday morning gatherings and educational classes in between, we barely have time to get people in and out. We just can not add anything else to the service, especially something so unpredictable.

7. It is new. We have never done it before.

8. The pastor can not pray for everyone in the church, and we do not have anyone else who is qualified to minister like that.

9. It will just stir up problems in the church and bring to light issues that we really do not want to deal with.

10. If we pray for people with problems, they will think we are condoning their sin. Besides, we really do not want to be around people with such disgraceful life habits.

Conduits of Grace

If you are going to establish an altar ministry time in your church, more than likely you will have to deal with at least a few of these objections, if not all of them. But as pastors and church leaders, addressing the fears and wrong attitudes head-on is best. It is up to us to educate our people about the importance and role of personal ministry and then foster an atmosphere of compassion where it can flourish.

One thing that we must keep in mind is that God is the power source, not us. Prayer was His idea and He makes it work. We do not have to produce anything ourselves, we just have to be "user friendly" to God, and He will come on the scene to touch lives. With one hand on the need, and the other to Him, we can be "conduits" of His love and mercy. But we have to be willing to *pray* the price. We might even have to be willing to stay past 12:00 and be persistent in prayer to see a breakthrough. We can not just throw up 30 second prayers that end with, "if it be your will...," and expect God to do miracles. We must commit to pray as long as it takes.

As I travel and speak to pastors, leaders, and laypeople about prayer, I love to give them a taste of personal ministry during the seminar. After a time of teaching, I ask the people to stand up, and I pray for them. I then instruct them to place their hand on the person in front of them and pray the first thing that comes to mind. I even encourage them to pray out loud if they feel comfortable doing so. I conclude by having each person find out what their partner prayed, and then we have an informal time of sharing.

It always amazes me (and them) how, in a room full of strangers, many people testify that the person behind them prayed in a specific manner for a real need in their life! They allow themselves to become conduits through which God pours out His love and grace. For some, it is the first time they have ever taken a chance on hearing God and allowed Him to minister through them. They are blessed as a result. They get excited because they realize that anyone can be a conduit, and the ideal of one-on-one ministry becomes a painless, almost enjoyable reality.

One Sure Sign

One sure sign of a church with a dynamic prayer ministry is an altar speckled with Kleenex boxes. I see it in churches of all types and sizes—Methodist, Baptist, Episcopal, Lutheran, Assemblies of God, charismatic, traditional, big, and small—good prayer ministries begin at the altar where individual needs can be lifted up. Personal ministry is the common denominator in praying churches, because it must be learned and modeled within the church itself before it can be turned outward.

As a pastor, I always set aside time during the services for people to receive individual prayer at the altar or in their seats. For the man I met on the airplane, or the lady who brought the handgun into my office, this would be the most important ten minutes in their week. The opportunity to share their pain with another believer, to be touched by the Father, and to receive compassion and healing, would mean more to them than the best sermon I ever preached. We enlisted laypeople who had a heart for this kind of ministry to be conduits, and they were always on call at the altar. During the time of personal prayer, I became a facilitator, and they became the ministers.

Altar Training

The success of altar ministry depends greatly on training. It is important that the people doing the praying are "commissioned" by the pastor to ensure that they are equipped for the task. Allowing someone who is not spiritually mature enough or who has the wrong motives to pray with people could do more harm than good. I suggest that you incorporate the following guidelines into your prayer team training:

1. You are at the altar to listen and pray. Do not be shocked by what you hear and do not judge.

2. You are not there to talk about yourself.

3. Ask for permission to pray.

4. Be aware of personal hygiene.

5. Men pray with men, women pray with women, couples pray with couples.

6. Listen to the Holy Spirit for direction. Use an appropriate point of contact such as laying on of hands or anointing with oil.

7. Have necessary materials on hand including your Bible, tissues, oil, prayer guides, scripture references and a name tag.

8. Pray the answer, not the problem. Do this by praying scripture based prayers.

9. Know when and where to refer people that need special attention such as someone who has just accepted Christ, someone who is suicidal, someone who is dealing with serious situations that might have legal implications, or someone who needs spiritual deliverance.

9. Take people who are very distressed or who just need an extended time of prayer into a designated place away from the sanctuary.

10. Make pertinent materials available to those who receive prayer.

What It Is Not

Almost as important as educating people about what altar ministry *is*, is educating them about what it is *not*. Emphasize the following boundaries:

1. Altar ministry is <u>not</u> a sign of weakness. People who come forward to receive prayer are simply bringing their problems to the throne and submitting themselves to God. If anything, it is a sign of spiritual strength because in our shortcomings, He can make provision known.

2. Altar ministry is <u>not</u> a counseling session. Workers are not trained or qualified to give advice or offer opinions and they should refrain from doing so, even if they are asked. They are trained to pray—nothing else.

3. Altar ministry is <u>not</u> a time for deliverance. Because of the nature of intense spiritual warfare, this type of prayer should not be carried out in a worship service in front of the entire con-

gregation. It is best done in more private settings under the supervision of several mature and experienced intercessors.

4. Altar ministry is <u>not</u> a show. The goal is not to entertain the congregation. Although emotions do tend to flow during these times of ministry, outbursts of tears or laughter are in no way a yardstick by which to measure the success of the ministry time.

5. Altar ministry is <u>not</u> a commitment to solve problems. Altar workers are under no obligation to *become* the answer to every need they encounter. Their job is simply to pray. God's job is to handle the outcome.

6. Altar ministry is <u>not</u> focused on the pastor. Although he or she may choose to pray with some people who come to the altar, the shepherd's main role should be to facilitate and oversee the ministry time. Having an adequate number of trained workers available to pray will help curb the temptation some may have to view this time as an opportunity to "bend the pastor's ear" about something.

7. Altar ministry is <u>not</u> a time to receive new members. These two important aspects of the worship service need to be kept separate so that one is not confused for the other. They are both vital, but they serve distinctively different purposes in the life of the church.

8. Altar ministry is <u>not</u> a big deal! Do not make it harder than it is. Although it will take some time to develop, personal ministry time can be as easy and natural as praise and worship. Once you have established it as a part of your services, you will wonder why you ever had church without it.

The First Altars

Back in the early Methodist camp meetings and revivals, the

focal point of prayer was the "mourner's bench," from whence we get our modern day altar rails. Accounts of these meetings indicate that believers spent much time on these rough benches praying for the lost to experience forgiveness, deliverance and spiritual renewal. They prayed with expectancy, and received the seekers as they responded to the gospel. Over time, however, as the role of prayer seemed to dwindle, the mourner's bench evolved into a symbolic structure where perhaps communion was given or new members were greeted. Today, in many churches, they are simply fences to keep me away from you and you away from me. How much more effective our churches would be if we could recapture the spirit of fervent prayer that once took place at the mourner's bench. John Wesley once said, "Prayer is a means of grace." As churches, let us be in the business of lavishing that grace on all those we can reach.

(Featured in the March/April 1996 issue of *Good News Magazine*)

Tales and Treasures

The Naked Truth

Terry tells this story about an important lesson they failed to teach him at seminary:

Early in my days as senior pastor of Aldersgate, three beautiful young ladies came to me wanting to be baptized. I was excited because they were three of our first converts, and they had come out of life styles of loose morals and promiscuity. I was so proud that they were turning their lives around, I wanted to make a big event out of the baptism service.

Because we were still meeting in an elementary school, we did not have a baptismal. So I asked the Baptist preacher if he would let me use his sanctuary on a Sunday evening for the special service. I was determined to really do it right, and they had plenty of space to accommodate my small congregation.

Now I had not ever baptized anyone by immersion before, least of all in a Baptist church, so when I saw the white robes hanging in the dressing area, I told the girls, "Take off your clothes so they won't get wet and put on those robes. When I call your name, just step down into the water towards me."

The service was moving; the atmosphere was perfect. It was time for the girls to make public their decisions to live for Christ and change their ways. But the moment I lowered the first one into the water, I knew I had made a terrible mistake!

I have no idea why they call them "modesty robes." There was nothing modest about them! The thin, white, gauze material left nothing to the imagination. As I looked down at the figure that I was imminently going to have to pull out of the water in front of my whole church, I almost swallowed my tongue. She started to fight a little bit, trying to come up for air, but all the feeling had suddenly been drained from my limbs. I felt paralyzed, so I did the only thing I could think of. I said abruptly, "Everyone bow your head in prayer!"

The worst part was that when she did come up and realize how she looked, she was not a bit embarrassed. She strutted up the steps and out of that baptismal, swinging everything she had, and I still had two to go!

Buried Alive

When Terry decided it was time to have a baptismal put in their new sanctuary, he wanted to make it different—creative. So he enlisted a carpenter in the church to build a large, rectangular, wooden box around a small Jacuzzi. He also requested that the box have a lid so that the baptismal could be covered when it was not being used. As a final touch, he asked the carpenter to put the whole thing on wheels so that it could be moved around the sanctuary as needed.

When it was completed, the work of art looked exactly like a beautifully hand-crafted casket. Terry christened it one Easter morning by placing it in the front of the church adorned with a full casket spray of flowers. He preached a message on the death, burial and resurrection of Jesus, and ended up baptizing more than thirty people that day—no modesty robes.

That unusual baptismal turned out to be one of the centerpieces of Aldersgate Church. Baptisms were a time of celebration. Friends and family members would gather around—especially the children—to take part in the occasion. Husbands stood beside wives; mothers stood beside children; friends stood with their peers. Sometimes people wept; other times they shouted for joy. Almost always there was singing and praise. The presence of the Holy Spirit was so strong during those moments that often two baptisms would turn into twelve. Terry, through his creativity and passion for the heart of God, did what he does best—he took something religious and made it real.

I think there's a book in your heart.

It's really great to be here today at...
where am I?

Where was I last week?

I belong to two churches—a white
church and an African-American
church. I can only take the white
church so long and then I have to
go get free.

Prayers for the lost are like
911 calls in heaven.

People want more from church than a
parking place, a three-point sermon and
a bulletin.

Some Methodists are so shy they won't
lead in silent prayer.

Prayer should not be a response
to crisis, but to Christ.

FOR HIS NAME'S SAKE

*Dr. Synan's message, as he spoke to a room full of United Methodist preachers and leaders, was that every great Holiness and Pentecostal movement could be traced back to what God did in the life of John Wesley and what he taught. He said emphatically that the "greatest spiritual forces in the founding of America were the Methodist circuit riders and the camp meetings that spread scriptural holiness all over these lands as Wesley told them to."
...He reminded us of our heritage of fiery camp meetings where people flocked to the altars seeking more of God, and he explained that at the turn of the century, we were the largest, fastest growing church in the world because of how God moved in those early tent revivals. ...He urged us to trace our spiritual history, not just our organizational history, to feel the heartbeat of our ancestry.*

Numbers 14 tells an interesting story about Moses and the Israelites. Upon hearing the report of the people that were inhabiting the Promised Land—they were of great size and very powerful—the Israelites were frightened and angry. They grumbled against Moses and Aaron, saying, "If only we had died in Egypt! Or in this desert! Why is the LORD bringing us to this land only to let us fall by the sword?" (v. 2-3). Even though they had witnessed miracle after miracle as God had led them to the land they were to inhabit, they were once again ready to choose a new leader and retreat back to the safety of captivity.

Then the Lord spoke to Moses, "How long will these people treat me with contempt? How long will they refuse to believe in me, in spite of all the miraculous signs I have performed among them? I will strike them down with a plague and destroy them..." (v. 11-12). God was so offended by the Israelites' lack of faith that He was ready to kill them all! But Moses, who probably felt like saying, "Go ahead, God. Take them all out," instead interceded for his people.

By going to God and pleading for them to be spared, Moses demonstrated how strong his relationship with God really was. But what is most interesting to me is the logic Moses used with God. He did not try to defend the Israelites' actions, nor did he call them names or try to disassociate from them. Moses simply reminded God of all that He had invested in these people and that *His* reputation was at stake. In essence, He said to God, "Everyone knows about these people you have led out of Egypt. All the nations have heard what is going on. If you put them to death here in the desert, what will people say about *you*, Lord?" **And the Lord replied, "I have forgiven them, as you asked"** (v. 20).

God has a lot invested in this United Methodist Church and in some sense, I believe it is *His* reputation that is now at stake. Think of all that our history entails: churches were birthed in nearly every county in America, our forefathers' passion for soul-winning resulted in millions of converts, we have raised billions of dollars to help those in need, we have taken bold stands against all kinds of social injustice. Most importantly, our denomination has a rich history of fervent prayer evangelism. The unmatched explosion of revival fire that spread throughout this country as part of the Methodist movement was a result of lifetimes spent in prayer by the early saints that have gone before us.

An article appeared in the August 9, 1993 edition of Newsweek magazine that caught my attention with the title, "Dead End for the Mainline?" ...The author cited membership figures for 1965 and for 1992 for what he called "liberal Protestantism's seven sister denominations [which included] the United Methodist Church. ...The losses were staggering, some denominations withering in size by almost fifty percent! If added together, the numbers showed that these seven churches, over the last 30 years, have seen 6.9 million people leave their flocks for other pastures.

Could it be that now our United Methodist Church, as well as other mainline denominations, are in a crisis of money and membership, identity and loyalty, because we have lost our passion for Jesus and His mandate to fulfill the Great Commission? ...Do we still have the Father's heart to reach this generation for Christ?

Even now, as we struggle with doctrinal issues and search to regain our lost identity, millions of people who live within walking distance of a local United Methodist church are facing an eternity in hell because they have yet to embrace the gospel. As we deal with turmoil, confusion and anger within our ranks, people sitting in our pews on Sunday mornings are in desperate need of a touch from God. In nearly every community I visit, seventy to eighty percent of the people are unchurched.

I am not suggesting that the issues we are facing are unimportant or that they do not need to be dealt with. They do, with boldness and in love. But perhaps there is a cancer that lies deeper than the question of homosexuality. Perhaps our sense of purpose has become splintered because we have forgotten what it means to be so wrapped up in Jesus that reaching the lost is all that really matters. Perhaps we have sailed into treacherous waters because we have lost our ability to steer.

In the heat of World War II, the Germans worked fervently behind closed doors constructing what they thought would be the greatest military weapon ever conceived. In mid 1941, they launched the battleship Bismarck, with an armored shell eighteen inches thick, and a gun that could hurl a shell the size of a Volkswagen over twenty miles. ...The Bismarck seemed impenetrable.

But not long after its impressive debut, the ultimate German weapon was spotted by a pair of enemy sea planes on patrol. Made partially of canvas, the planes carried only one torpedo each, since they were not designed to be aggressive attack planes. As they flew over the battleship, they both fired their torpedoes.

...Little did they know that the second torpedo had, in fact, knocked the rudder of the Bismarck off its hinges, and without a rudder, the mighty fortress was left with no way to steer. Although the damage seemed totally insignificant, the most powerful, indestructible military force ever created was actually helpless in the water. Within hours, it had floated directly into the middle of a British fleet, which shelled it again and again until the great ship went down.

Prayer is our rudder. Without it, we have no ability to steer and no sense of direction. As a denomination, are we praying the price? Are we united in prayer across the nation, affecting our cities for Him? Are we praying constantly for renewed vision and sense of purpose? In our local churches, how many of our members are committed to ongoing prayer ministries? How many of our churches are seeing professions of faith on a regular basis? How much time is spent at the monthly preachers' meetings in prayer? What about at Annual Conferences?

The one thing Jesus desired for the church was that it be a "house of prayer" (Matthew 21:13). All of our other activities, as important as they may be, must never be allowed to squeeze out the most powerful, life-changing, soul-winning thing we can do as a church. John Wesley believed that God does nothing except in answer to prayer, so if we are to see a mighty move of God in this Church, we must get on our knees.

In the two hundred years of our existence, we have never had a national call to prayer, and we are long overdue. I believe, as do many others, that the only answer to the many problems plaguing our denomination is a return to our Wesleyan heritage of tenacious prayer evangelism. We need a wake-up call! More radical than reorganizing our polity, more extreme than adopting a new hymnal, our solution is a corporate call back to a radical dependency on God.

Having written the book, *Pray the Price: United Methodists United in Prayer*, I am now traveling full time heralding this message to local churches, districts, and conferences across the country. Whether you are a United Methodist or simply a Christian who would like to see revival sweep through mainline churches, you can become a part of this call to prayer in three ways:

First, begin praying with us at noon every Thursday for God to pour out His Spirit on our denomination and on the other mainline churches. We call this "Pray Down at High Noon," and are working to enlist one million United Methodists to pray. If you are not ready to give up on these spiritual giants, start praying the price to invite a new move of God that we could see an awakening in this generation.

Second, find out if your church has a prayer coordinator and support him or her in any way you can. If your church does not have a person dedicated to the task of promoting prayer, work with your pastor to try and appoint one. Leadership in the prayer movement is critical. One of our purposes is to motivate churches to appoint prayer coordinators, and then work closely with those appointed as they build prayer ministries.

Finally, if your church does not have a prayer room—a place set aside especially for scheduled intercession—talk with your pastor about the possibility of starting one. We would like to see prayer rooms in every United Methodist Church in America so that we can truly walk out becoming a "house of prayer."

I do not think that God is finished with the United Methodist Church. He will not allow the lives of John Wesley, Francis Asbury, William Arthur, John Fletcher and many others to be for naught. As I remember our past, I look to the future, not with despair, but with hope and anticipation of how God is working among us. Now more than ever He is calling us to pray a new price and invite the Spirit to again ignite the revival fire that once burned with intensity. Many around the world are already experiencing incredible moves of God, and I do not want us to be left out. God will honor the prayers of His people, even a remnant. What we may perceive to be calamity, God can redeem for His own purpose.

Perhaps, like Moses, we need to repent for the ways in which all of us have grieved the heart of God due to pride, self-sufficiency and prayerlessness, and beseech Him to pour out His Spirit on us, not for our own sake, but for **His Name's sake**.

Excerpts taken from
Pray the Price: United Methodists United in Prayer

(Featured in the July/August 1998 issue of **Good News Magazine**)

Tales and Treasures

Open Mouth, Insert Foot

One of the perils of public speaking is that every time you stand up in front of a group of people, you run the risk of putting your foot in your mouth. Actually, in some cases, it can be more like your whole leg.

One subject that seems to give Terry more trouble than most is that of using "politically correct" language in reference to various people groups such as women, Asians, United Methodists, the elderly or the physically challenged. In total innocence, he is likely to refer to these same groups as girls, Chinese people, Methodists (a big no-no to those who remember the denominational merger), old people and handicapped. It is not that Terry looks upon any of these groups of people with an attitude of superiority—in fact, it is just the opposite.

Recently, however, we were listening at a prayer conference to Terry tell the story of a church that was doing some really amazing altar ministry. He was describing a scene at the altar, trying to convey how remarkably this particular church ministry had broken all barriers of race, age and economic status thanks to the pastor's humility and leadership. What actually came out of his mouth was something like, "...they were all at the altar—African-Americans, Hispanics, homeless...." We understood what he meant, but the combination had the wrong overtones.

After the session, as a small group of us were standing around in a break room drinking coffee, we gently brought up the issue. We were concerned that Terry might not have been aware that he had made such a potentially offensive statement. We were surprised, though, that he was well aware of the mistake.

"I knew I had messed up as soon as I spoke the words," he said. "But I couldn't think fast enough to redeem it. The only thing that kept coming to mind was to add 'and poorly dressed white people' to the list!"

The Salesman

When he was pastoring, Terry often joked about how his church staff would never let him have the checkbook. This was for good reason. He loves to give things away—money, books, his time—he would have spent every penny in the account.

Not too long ago he was attending a key United Methodist gathering just to promote the call to prayer, sell books and make some contacts. With over 1,000 people in attendance, he thought it would be time well spent, despite the fact that he was not on the speaking platform.

When he arrived at the convention center, however, he was ushered to the basement where the book tables were located. It was poorly lit and a little musty, and only a handful of stragglers wandered around looking at books. The other people who were selling looked bored, and one of them shook his head as Terry set down a box, saying, "Sales are terrible; we haven't moved a thing."

Terry thought about it for a moment. The basement was pretty dismal. He had a better idea.

He carried all of his book cases up to the main floor and stacked them right outside the doors to the ballroom where a session was just about to let out. Within a few minutes, people began pouring out of the double doors, and Terry went to work.

"Free books! Get your free book here!"

By the time the room had emptied, a pile of cardboard boxes lay by the door and there was not a single book to be found. It was not clear who enjoyed the frenzy more—those who were surprised by an unexpected free gift or the one doing the giving.

As he drove off, Terry thought about the dreary scene in the basement, "Must have been the location. I got rid of everything I brought!"

I have the gift of offense and it is
fully operational today.

This is good preachin'—
I'm glad I came!

Grandkids are God's reward for
not killing your own.

I love preaching in black churches because they help you when you preach.
White people just look at you. In a
black church, even when the sermon is
bad, they say, "Help him, Lord!"

How can we honor God, whom we can't see, if we can not honor His representative, whom we can see?

Pastors, do you ever wonder if spiritual resistance is real? Why do you think it takes a three-hour nap to recover from a 20 minute sermon?

There is no such thing as a bad prayer.

United Methodists are the most Christian denomination in the world. We give away 50,000 members a year to churches like yours.

7

"HOLY JEHOSHAPHAT! WE NEED TO PRAY!"

The "ites" were attacking—Moabites, Ammonites and Meunites. Collectively, we might call them the "Parasites," and they were moving toward Jerusalem with schemes and ability to wipe out Jehoshaphat and his men. They were a vast army, powerful and well-equipped, and they had misguided political viewpoints, I'm sure.

Jehoshaphat was alarmed. He knew the Israelites were dramatically outnumbered and would surely be defeated if they engaged in battle. But he was a godly king who was wise in the ways of the Lord. So rather than panicking or trying to turn the Parasites away by engaging them in a nasty, verbal war and voting against them, he called his people together to pray. In response, they came from "every town in Judah" to seek the Lord (2 Chronicles 20:4).

Jehoshaphat stood before his people in the courtyard of the temple and prayed:

O Lord, God of our fathers, are you not the God who is in heaven? You rule over all the kingdoms of the nations. Power and might are in your hand and no one can withstand you.... "...If calamity comes upon us, whether the sword of judgment, or plague or famine, we will stand in your presence before this temple that bears your Name and will cry out to you in our distress, and you will hear us and save us."

...O our God, will you not judge them [the Parasites]? For we have no power to face this vast army that is attacking us. We do not know what to do, but our eyes are upon you (2 Chronicles 20:6, 9, 12).

As the Israelites held a prayer vigil there before the Lord, the Holy Spirit spoke through a prophet and said to them:

"Do not be afraid or discouraged because of this vast army. For the battle is not yours, but God's" (2 Chronicles 20:15).

Could it be that since the battle was not really the Israelites', then perhaps the Parasites were not really the enemy, either?

As the Lord had instructed them to do, the Israelites took their positions and stood firm. Jehoshaphat bowed with his face to the ground, and his people fell down in worship. They sang and praised the Lord with loud voices, and as they did, they watched the Moabites, Ammonites and Meunites turn and begin killing each other until the Parasite army was completely self-destroyed.

The Battle

Today, our United Methodist denomination is under attack. "Parasites" are eating away at the vitality and peace of our Church. Most tragically, the conflict has us so preoccupied that we are unable to concentrate on the business of sharing Jesus with those who have not met Him. We are drained, divided and distracted.

On many fronts, the battle has robbed us of our excitement and passion for the purposes of God.

Just like Jehoshaphat and his men, many of us have scanned the battlefield and labeled "enemy" anyone who appears to be at odds with us. We have identified all those who are facing a different direction, even if it is slight, and we have made them our adversaries. We are pointing fingers at Bishops, seminaries, pastors and other renewal groups, convinced that our denomination would make a quick and dramatic recovery if only they would think like us.

But we have failed to correctly identify both the battle and the enemy. The true battle is not over issues but eternity. Our enemies are not brothers and sisters in Christ, but powers and principalities of darkness. We are engaged in spiritual warfare over thousands of souls that still hang in the balance between heaven and hell. And spiritual war calls for spiritual weapons.

Our Response – Prayer

I meet pastors and laypeople every week who desperately want to see a move of God in this Church. But like Jehoshaphat, they feel that the situation is hopeless. The more we debate, the hotter the issues become; and with every vote that is cast, opposing sides become more and more entrenched.

Many are expecting the General Conference in May 2000 to be a pivotal event in our denomination. Because of this, and in response to the urgency of the hour, we need to pray. It is important that we follow Jehoshaphat's example by humbling ourselves and focusing our eyes on God, not the problems. "We do not know what to do, but our eyes are upon you" (2 Chronicles 20:12). We need to pray continually for our leaders and our Church, but more specifically for the spiritual battle that will be waged in Cleveland next year. Like the Israelites who sought the Lord and relinquished the battle to Him, it is time to take up our positions in Christ, relying on His promises, and see His deliverance at hand. We do not have to save the Church or defeat the devil; instead, we can march to the tune of His victory over evil. The battle is simply not ours to fight.

For the first time that I am aware of, several groups within our denomination including Good News, Aldersgate Renewal and the Confessing Movement have all come together to facilitate a concerted prayer effort during General Conference. We hope to have 2,000 prayer delegates there, elected by the Holy Spirit, claiming spiritual victory for this United Methodist Church. Although we do not know all of the specifics at this time, our plans include at least three types of prayer:

1. Prayer Room – Just as the Israelites stood in the presence of God, prayer delegates will quietly wait before the Lord in a prayer room. They can be still, meditate and listen for direction, or intercede in teams for the decisions being made. Our goal is for this room to be occupied 24 hours a day for the entire session.

2. Prayerwalking – The Lord instructed the Israelites to march, and so prayer delegates will "march" throughout the conference center, hotels and even restaurants. They will cover the entire downtown area by walking and praying, claiming an atmosphere of faith and not fear, hope and not discouragement.

3. On-Site Prayer – Prayer delegates may elect to sit in the gallery during the main sessions and pray silently.

Throughout General Conference, we will ask prayer delegates to maintain an attitude of praise. It must be evident both in our actions and on our faces. The last thing we want is to have people there in the name of prayer spreading doom and gloom! This is very important for several reasons. First, since we know that God is in control of the outcome, we can walk by faith in His victory. Second, joy is contagious and we need to keep in mind that we have much to be thankful about. Third, there is no room for pride or arrogance in this mission. We are there to humbly bow before the Lord as Jehoshaphat did. In fact, in the latter part of 2 Chronicles 20, the Israelites modeled four different forms of praise, indicating how important this element was to their appropriation of the victory. They bowed (v. 18), praised God with loud voices (v. 19), sang (v. 21) and gave thanks (v. 21). We can sing and shout at appropriate times, or quietly worship and offer thanks as we pray in the prayer room or walk the halls. But we must continually praise God, for He inhabits the praises of His people and it is His presence that we desire at this meeting and in our Church.

God's Response?

Although there will be many specific requests to pray about during General Conference, I believe we need to look for three outcomes: (1) for any evil strongholds or assignments to be broken; (2) for the voting delegates to hear God and (3) for a bold vision for the Great Commission to come forth.

I do not know what God has in store for this denomination, and I do not know how He will answer our prayers. But I do know that if we are willing to seek Him and place the battle completely in His hands, He will deliver us from the schemes of the evil one and bring glory to the name of Jesus. We do not have to know the end of the story, because the battle belongs to the Lord. We just have to be faithful to pray.

(Featured in the November/December 1999 issue of *Good News Magazine*)

Tales and Treasures

Reckless for God

Lots of words have been used to describe Terry's ministry style, but "bashful" is not one of them. He will pray at any time, in any place, for just about anything. In his younger days, before he had the wisdom gained from years of ministry, he might have even described himself as "reckless for God."

In his early days in rural churches, he pastored a lot of farmers and ranchers. One Sunday afternoon as he was driving home from church, he passed by a farm owned by one of his parishioners. Coincidentally, the man was kneeling by the side of the road, just inside of his fence. As Terry got closer, he could see that the man was stooped over a cow that was lying in the grass. He stopped his car and got out.

"What's wrong, Harold? I noticed you weren't in church today."

"Anthrax," he said. There's been an outbreak of it around here, preacher. I've already lost several head, and I'm about to lose this one."

"Well let me pray for her," Terry said, taking off his coat and loosening his tie.

"You mean you're gonna pray for a cow?"

"Sure," Terry said enthusiastically. "God made the

cattle on a thousand hills—I'll bet he could heal this one."

With that, he bent down in the grass, put his hands on the cow's head, and began to pray. He took authority over the disease, prayed against the spirit of death and in Jesus' name rebuked anything he could think of that could make a cow sick. He prayed with boldness and passion. Harold looked on, without saying a word.

When he finished praying, Terry looked down at the motionless cow, hoping she would begin to stir immediately. But instead, she looked back up at him with her big brown eyes, let out one last "Hmmph!" and died right there at his feet.

Terry got up, brushed himself off and shuffled back to his car. Too embarrassed to look Harold in the eyes, he simply got in his car and drove away.

Harold just stood there, without saying a word.

Every Body

Gregg Parris, pastor of Union Chapel United Methodist Church in Muncie, IN and long time friend of Terry tells this story:

A few years ago, I was having dinner with Terry and several other pastors. The waitress serving us was young and very beautiful. She was, you know, nicely put together.

During the course of the meal, as she came to the table and left, a noticeable tension hung in the air. As "holy men of God," none of us wanted to let the others know that we had noticed anything in particular about the waitress. But of course, everyone had.

As we were finishing, she came to the table again to clear away some of the plates.

"Anyone save room for dessert?" she asked.

We all shifted uneasily in our seats and fumbled with our napkins. Terry answered, "No thank you—just a check."

As she left the table again, his eyes followed her and he said out loud, "God has made everything."

"Yes," we all affirmed, "God made everything."

"And God made everybody," Terry continued.

"That's right, Terry. God made everybody."

Then Terry thought for a minute, glanced back over to the doorway from which the young waitress kept appearing, and said, "And God made some bodies especially well!"

In that moment of great laughter and relief, all of our false piety and presumption was exposed and melted by Terry's quick wit, sense of humor, and unique ability to creatively state the obvious.

I practice time-release humor—you'll
get that later.

I'm gonna take you on the road with me.

If you don't get goosebumps, you need
to get your goosebumper fixed.

How many does this church sleep?

I don't think God is through with the
United Methodist Church.

Jesus said, "Come to me,"
but He went to them.

Somewhere along the way, prayer and
evangelism got a divorce.

We need to pray prayers commensurate
with the size of our God.

TAKING GOD TO WORK

"Five Shot in Office Complex!"

"Three Gunned Down in Factory!"

"Ten Injured in Downtown Rampage!"

The headlines tell the story. This country, once known as the "land of opportunity," is fast becoming the land of the stressed out, on-the-edge employee who might, at any moment, walk into the office and unload years of frustration through the barrel of a semiautomatic handgun. We see it on the evening news far too often—a public workplace turned battleground because someone "just couldn't take it any more."

I was in a retail store not long ago waiting at the service desk to return an item. The only customer at the register, I stood there trying not to appear too impatient as I waited for the sales clerk to finish what was obviously a personal phone call. She was flustered, and it did not take me long to realize why. She apparently had a little boy or girl that was sick and needed to be picked up from day care. Her boss, however, would not let her go because the store was busy and another worker had failed to show up. By the time she hung up the phone and turned to help me, she was on the verge of tears.

Her situation is representative of the equation many people face in the work world—struggling to balance the stuff of life against the need for a paycheck, knowing all the while that getting ahead on one side always means sacrificing on the other. Any parent who works outside the home understands this dilemma especially well. And too often, the sum total of the equation is stress, anxiety or despair. The result can be anything from a momentary emotional breakdown to a calculated violent act.

Trends in the Workplace

But balancing work and family life is not the only problem creating stress in the workplace. In most any job, from the highest levels of management to the lowest minimum wage positions, several factors are at work.

1. Longer work hours - As Americans, we are spending more and more time each year in the workplace, over 160 hours more per year compared with two decades ago, according to economist Juliet Schor. With competition fierce for good jobs, we can not afford to be the one found slacking off. As a result, we are increasingly more inclined to wrap our lives around the people and events related to work. We eat, socialize, date and even exercise at the office—we are a society full of individuals gaining our identities based on what we do.

2. Pressure to perform - As with every area of life, the office is an easy place to fall into the comparison trap. We work hard for a better position, a higher promotion, a bigger office and a fatter paycheck. It is easy to get discouraged when you see mirages of greener pastures all around.

3. Impersonal, uncaring atmosphere - The work world seems like a hostile place at times, where the almighty dollar steers the boat without any concern for who might be hanging over the edge. A family crisis or personal illness will probably get you a day off, but not necessarily with the boss's blessing. While some employers make every effort to support workers through personal trials, others make no effort at all.

4. Job insecurity - The days of working 25 or 30 years with one company are virtually gone. Most people today change jobs several times during their working years, sometimes even changing occupations. Small businesses are always on tenuous financial ground and large companies are prone to lay-offs and factory closings. It is not uncommon to hear someone talking about a skill or trade that they can "fall back on" in case their present employment falls through.

5. Greed - Whereas a few decades ago, there were actually companies that still existed for the primary purpose of serving or helping their customers, today that animal seems like a dying breed. The bottom line matters more than a job well done. With our economy booming and the average family income rising, the phrase "enough money" has become sort of an oxymoron.

6. Ever-changing technology - The speed at which technology changes and updates makes it very hard for businesses and workers to stay current and competitive. The skills a worker gained in school or training are likely to be obsolete within just a few years, just as equipment purchased today will not give a business owner the edge he wants a few tax returns down the road. Trying to keep pace with technology can be a stressful, costly struggle.

Spiritual Receptivity

I recently read an article in November 8, 1999 issue of *BusinessWeek* magazine that described yet another trend in the workplace. It could be an outgrowth of those I have already mentioned, or an extension of larger social phenomenon and new ways of thinking. Either way, I found it fascinating. It was strong confirmation of what I already sensed to be true.

The article, entitled "Religion in the Workplace," stated that "a spiritual revival is sweeping across Corporate America. Gone is the old taboo," it said, "against talking about God at work." In fact, according to Gallup, when Americans were asked if they had occasion to talk about their religious faith at work in the past 24 hours, 48% said, "Yes."

Although author Michelle Conlin did not limit her discussion to one faith in particular, many of the examples she described involve Bible-believing Christianity. Consider the following testimonies she cited to the fact that God has "gone to work"!

- Companies such as Pizza Hut, Taco Bell and Wal-Mart are hiring chaplains (some through a nonprofit called Marketplace Ministries) to make regular visits to their franchises and offer spiritual support to workers for just about any reason. They can even perform weddings or funerals.

- In Minneapolis, Minnesota, 150 heavy hitters meet monthly to listen to Christian chief executives offer business solutions from the Bible.

- In Boston, Massachusetts, another group of big-league corporate minds meets together regularly for an invitation-only prayer breakfast called "First Tuesday."

- An organization called Fellowship for Companies for Christ International says there are over 10,000 Bible and prayer groups meeting regularly in workplaces across the country.

- Today, there are about 30 different conferences on spirituality in the workplace compared to only one just five years ago.

- Several universities have opened research centers dedicated to learning about religion in the workplace.

- The number of related books in print on the subject has quadrupled since 1990 to 79 last year.

In general, openness to prayer, faith and God is on the rise throughout our society. Gallup's poll found that 95% of Americans say they believe in God or some "universal spirit'" while 51% say they would like to spend more time enjoying God and praying. With more people looking for meaning in life through their faith, it is only natural that they are carrying that spiritual hunger with them to their job sites.

Where's the Church?

The *Business Week* article went on to describe the life of Kim, a Taco Bell cashier with "a husband in prison, a daughter in rehab and two mouths to feed at home." Kim explained how she relies on the corporate chaplain, saying "A lot of times, I get real depressed, and I have to talk to somebody, or I'll explode. If I didn't have that support, I don't know what I'd do."

As I read her story, so typical of many, my first thought was, "How wonderful. God bless Taco Bell for being willing to minister to its employees." My next thought, however, was an alarming

"Where is the local church in this picture? Why in the world does Taco Bell have to hire a regional chaplain to minister to Kim when she probably passes by at least two or three Christian churches on her way to work every day?" The irony of it disturbed me.

I am convinced that as church members, we need to pull our heads out of the guacamole and smell the burritos! Our communities are full of "Kims" that work in dry cleaners, beauty salons, banks, day care centers, retail stores, convenience shops, factories and office buildings. They cook food, repair cars, pick up garbage, build houses, teach children and run computers. They may even sit next to us in the pew on Sunday morning, unless they have to work.

But Monday through Saturday, while they are negotiating the demands of life, they are as far out of our reach as they can be. Hurting, depressed and discouraged, they have nowhere to turn unless they are fortunate enough to work for a company like Taco Bell that is doing what it can to address spiritual and emotional needs. It is as if we welcome them in to a worship service, feed them a dose of religion, and then send them back through the mysterious veil that separates church from market. A week later, they reappear through the haze for another shot of strategy and a pat on the back.

Prayer Force in the Workplace

OK. So the workplace is volatile because people are on edge. And at the same time, or perhaps because of that, those in the work force are more receptive to the things of God than ever before. I have said all that to say this: it is time that we mobilize a prayer force for the workplace. We have organized prayer for pastors and politicians. We have raised up intercessors for public schools and unevangelized nations. We have even coordinated prayer efforts for every zip code and every home in America. Now what about every business? The stage is set. It is time to let go of the idea that the church is not relevant to the marketplace and get serious about praying and ministering to the needs of those in it. Where prayer groups and Bible studies are already thriving, revival may not be far behind.

Jesus had no problem mixing ministry and commerce. He often moved through the marketplaces, healing, touching and praying for people. He understood the world of business, having worked as a carpenter for many years with his father. He no doubt knew what it was like to buy materials, balance a budget, collect receivables and manage time. Remember? He even paid taxes. He often related His teachings to the livelihoods of His listeners, and the principles He taught were as applicable to the fisherman as they were to the woman weaving clothing or the man selling baskets. Although he told hurting people, "Come to me," He really went to them.

God wants the lazy checker at your grocery store to know the depths of His love. He wants to heal the chain-smoking, long-haired construction worker who was injured on the job. He wants to lavish grace upon the corporate officer who is embezzling money to keep up with a mortgage. He wants to meet sinners at the point of their needs to bring glory to Himself and salvation to all who will call upon His name.

As we make ourselves the conduits of saving grace by offering to pray for the needs of hurting people, something else miraculous happens. God puts His heart in us for the lives of those around us. He instills in us a holy compassion that can transcend our own humanity and enable us to see people as He sees them. The more we pray, the more we will want to pray as we sense His burden for the lost who are dying in their sin.

Giving Living

But praying for the needs of people in the workplace is only half the picture. We can also pray for the businesses themselves to prosper so that again, people will be drawn unto Him and He will be worshipped as the Provider. God never intended for His creation to toil in vain. His desire is for all to be blessed and know the joy of "giving living."

God's original plan for Adam and Eve was abundance and prosperity—what we might call "the good life." When He created them, He made them managers of the family estate, the Garden of Eden, which was a plush paradise where all their needs were met. They happily tended the garden, and in return, it bore a king's share of the ripest, sweetest fruit. "Work" was pleasurable because they had no worries, no lack, no straining to make a buck—everything they could possibly want was at their disposal. This was the way God intended life to be.

But Adam and Eve broke the rules. They did the one and only thing which they had been instructed not to do. And when they bit into the apple, they lost a lot more than their innocence. They lost control of the Garden with all of its abundance, as well as access to God's checkbook. They subleased the estate to a miserly scoundrel named Satan, forfeiting their thrones for thorns. Their fall set in motion the curse of poverty.

From that moment on, Adam and Eve and all their descendants (you and I) would not have things so easy. Labor would be painful and survival would be a struggle. The earth would produce thorns and thistles, and only by the sweat of their brows would Adam and Eve be able to make it give forth the fruit that had once grown plentiful in the Garden. They would discover want, greed and eventually, credit.

Luckily, God had a backup plan. First, He entered into a covenant with a man named Abraham (Genesis 15). He promised to give Abraham more descendants than there are stars in the sky, and he assured Abraham that his descendants would form a great nation. God made a way to pour out His blessing on all the nations of the earth through this one man. The seed for "giving living" was planted.

God's plan of restoration and redemption culminated in Jesus, born into the earth as the "last Adam." The perfect model of Spirit in the flesh, Jesus was the epitome of giving living, a blessing going somewhere to happen. Everywhere He went, He did good. He gave love, healing, life, forgiveness, truth, hope, peace and joy. He was God's show and tell for the life of abundance.

Jesus's death on the cross sealed the New Covenant between God and man. His body was broken in order to break the curse of death and poverty. He bore the crown of thorns on His head so that God might restore the crown of blessing to yours and mine. The Bible says, "For you know the grace of our Lord Jesus Christ, that though he was rich, yet for your sakes he became poor, so that you through his poverty might become rich" (2 Corinthians 8:9). As a result of the exchange at the cross, "God is able to make all grace abound to you, so that in all things at all times, having all that you need, you will abound in every good work" (2 Corinthians 9:8).

The Apostle Paul summed it up like this, "Christ redeemed us from the curse of the law by becoming a curse for us, for it is written: 'Cursed is everyone who is hung on a tree.' He redeemed us in order that the blessing given to Abraham might come to the Gentiles through Jesus Christ, so that by faith we might receive the promise of the Spirit" (Galatians 3:13-14).

The blessings of Abraham are ours through Jesus! This is very significant because it means that we can ask God to bless us, even financially, since we know that it is truly His desire to do so. He wants to abundantly bless the work of our hands so that we can "abound in every good work." He blesses us to be a blessing to others. We can live out of Him and experience the same bountiful provision that Adam and Eve first experienced in the Garden. We can practice giving living.

The Prayer Box

As a way to help churches penetrate the workplace with prayer, we have developed a Prayer Box Kit that equips an individual or a family to adopt a business in their area. The Kit comes complete with a drawing style prayer box that is placed in the business to receive prayer requests, a training booklet with step by step instructions for the box sponsor and prayer guides for both personal needs and businesses. It is exactly what a church needs to raise up a prayer force in the workplace with integrity and effectiveness.

Is there a business where you live that you would be willing to pray over for three months? Could you invite the Holy Spirit to transform the drugstore by your house or the fitness center where you work out? Could you sponsor a box in the teachers' lounge of your local high school in honor of the recent violent tragedies in schools across the nation?

As this ministry has been developing in various cities, the testimonies have been powerful. One sponsor received a request in her box, which was placed in her favorite restaurant, that said, "I am 72 years old and I am dying. I want to know if God is real." She was actually able to call the person and lead him to Christ right over the phone. In several cases, business owners have also responded to the gospel or have decided to give church another try because for the first time, they experienced God's love for them in a meaningful way.

The work force is ripe for harvest. People are more receptive to prayer than ever and they are searching for the deeper meaning of life that can only be found through Jesus Christ. But the world offers a host of deceptive substitutes. We as Christians can not afford to sit back and wait for the 80% of our cities' populations who are lost and unchurched to come to us. We must open our eyes to the need and take the Answer to the marketplace.

For more information about the Prayer Box Kit, contact
Prayer Point Press at 1 (888) 656-6067.

(Unpublished, 2000)

Tales and Treasures

The Room

"It's the second door on the right," the young woman said as she ushered Terry back to their guest bedroom. He was doing a seminar in a small town with few hotels, so one of the couples in the church had offered their home as a place for him to stay.

That night, as he lay in the darkness of the small room, he kept envisioning a nursery—baby crib against the wall, changing table under the window, toys scattered across the floor. Although he knew the couple had no children, he could not get the picture out of his mind.

The next morning as he sat with them eating breakfast, he could not help but mention the strange vision. "A funny thing happened last night," he started, "as I was trying to get to sleep. I kept seeing baby things around the room, as if it were a nursery. Does that mean anything to you?"

Both of them looked shocked. They glanced at each other and then back at Terry. Sadness registered on the woman's face, as her husband began to explain, "We have been trying for several years to have a baby. The doctors don't even seem to know why we can't— my wife and I are both healthy. Recently we've been praying that God would make us content without children. I guess we've kind of given up. That room you were sleeping in would have been the baby's room."

Terry apologized for bringing up a painful topic and then said, "Could I pray for you?" With compassion and wisdom, He prayed God's grace and provision over the couple and pronounced a special blessing on them and their home.

You can probably imagine the end of the story. About one year later, Terry received the birth announcement in the mail with a handwritten letter of gratitude and praise to God. Though he does not remember much about the seminar that he taught that day, his attentive spirit and sensitivity to the heart of God made quite a difference in at least three lives in that small town.

Sunday Shoes

One of the topics that Terry often teaches about is the relationship between prayer and the worship service. He contends that most people who go to church show up on Sunday mornings a few minutes before the music starts, flop down in their seat, frazzled and distracted, and then somehow expect the pastor to "religion" them. He uses this story to illustrate the typical frame of mind of many churchgoers:

When our kids were little, Kay and I were driving to church one Sunday after having one of "those" mornings. Every parent knows that Satan can possess your sweet little angels in strange ways in the tumultuous hours before worship.

My son Travis, who was about six at the time, finally pushed me over the edge while we were in the car. I pulled over to the side of road, drug him out of the back seat, and applied some serious discipline to his back side. As I lovingly ushered him back into the car, resisting the urge to leave him standing right there on the shoulder, I bellowed, "If I hear one more word out of you before we get to church, I'll... I'll..." I did not really know what I would do, but he was pretty sure it would not be good.

Several quiet minutes later, as we piled out of the car in the church parking lot, I noticed that Travis only had one shoe on.

"Son, where is your other shoe?" I asked slowly.

"With fear and trepidation in his voice, he answered, "It fell off when you spanked me."

"And why didn't you say something?" I asked, knowing that my face was turning red and the veins on my neck were popping out.

"You told me not to say another word, Dad!"

Listen!

That sounds almost Christian.

Why would God send revival through the mainline churches? To humble the Charismatics.

I was in that church three years one Sunday!

When you ask God to fill you up, He asks, "How far do you want to go?" If you're content to idle in the station, He'll just give you a little squirt.

A Kleenex box is a sign of the Holy Spirit.

Church is one of the few organizations that exists for the sake of its non-members.

The Lord tattooed five words on my heart, "Build the church in prayer."